There, amid a pile of unconscious lancers, stood a man clad entirely in black. A dark cloak billowed about him. A familiar mask partially obscured his face, but it was the roguish smile that told them all that Zorro had indeed returned from the dead. He gazed up in wonder from his place on the floor. Zorro held a sword in one hand, a pistol in the other. Some of the soldiers glanced uneasily over their shoulders at the dark spot in the ceiling. They were certain the ghostly voice had emanated from there.

"We were just lamenting your passing, Zorro," Gutierrez replied, making a great effort to appear brave. "Put down the gun and fight me fairly so that we may mourn your passing properly."

Zorro accepted what he thought was a minimal challenge. He quickly sheathed his sword and extended his hand to the stranger, "Stand my friend."

Gutierrez advanced toward Zorro.

Their swords clashed and locked. Zorro's grin reflected no strain in holding the larger man back. After a moment, he pushed the lancer off balance. Zorro admonished, "I would have hoped my return would be met with a more earnest effort. . . . A cup of water, barkeep," Zorro asked coolly, as if ordering a drink during a swordfight was perfectly normal. "Fill it to the brim!" The barkeep rose from behind the bar where he had been cowering like a cub. "Come now," Zorro urged, not looking back. He was automatically defending himself against blow after blow from Gutierrez. His smile had not wavered a bit. Finally, the barkeep filled another cup with fresh water and held it out.

"You mock me!" Gutierrez roared and lunged. Zorro deftly stepped to the right.

"Then your mind is quicker than your blade after all!" laughed Zorro.

DAVID BERGANTINO

ZORRO

AND THE
DRAGON RIDERS

FORGE®

A TOM DOHERTY ASSOCIATES BOOK
NEW YORK

This is a work of fiction. All the characters and events portrayed in this book are either products of the author's imagination or are used fictitiously.

ZORRO AND THE DRAGON RIDERS

A Forge Book
Published by Tom Doherty Associates, Inc.
175 Fifth Avenue
New York, NY 10010

Forge® is a registered trademark of Tom Doherty Associates, Inc.

ISBN: 0-812-56768-4

First edition: March 1999

Printed in the United States of America

0 9 8 7 6 5 4 3 2 1

For the believers:

my parents,
Regina, Michael, Craig, Kendall, Patrick, Dawn, Jeff,
and the gang at Dalt's.

Chapter 1

"The fox has gone to his den to die!" shouted the tall young soldier, a bottle of tequila raised in a hearty salute.

In answer, a raucous cheer burst from the other soldiers gathered, and nearly a dozen more arms were raised, bottles and mugs crashing together, clanks and clunks filling the air, adding to the din. Shadows cast by sputtering torchlight played upon the cantina wall in a frenzied puppet show. The soldiers were in spirits finer than any tequila they could afford on their meager pay. Just as well, since for every gulp of alcohol, nearly half had found its way down their faces, soaking into their clothes, making the cantina air thick and humid, oppressive with the mingled odors of *cerveza* and wine and tequila and sweat.

"It is a shame, really," sighed Sergeant Garcia heavily from his seat at the head of one long wooden table, its surface worn smooth by years of supporting the elbows and boots of drunken revelers. Alcohol was making the sergeant philosophical. Well, as philosophical as the man ever got. He shifted his ponderous bulk—responsible on its own for much of the cantina's repugnant atmosphere—and stared at his beer mug, frowning. The mug was empty. "A double shame," he repeated.

Gutierrez, the soldier who had made the original toast, took a lengthy swig from his tequila and eyed the fat sergeant. Not just corpulent, thought Gutierrez. Nothing as dainty as hefty. Fat. *Muy gordo*. He stepped off the table from which he had made his bold toast.

"You find it a shame that the fox, El Zorro, might actually be gone?" Gutierrez squeezed into a seat directly across from Garcia, nearly having to fold himself in half to look the sergeant in the eyes. For this reason, he would stand most nights, leading cheers. His long legs accounted for much of his height—his knees scraped against the undersides of the tables when sitting, making him feel cramped and awkward. Better to stand as a giant among his peers.

Garcia's dull, wet eyes blinked emptily at the lancer. Gutierrez reminded the sergeant of his sister-in-law's yappy little dog, and sometimes of a cur who chewed furniture and dug holes in floors. He was rash, arrogant, and a nuisance, but the young man was also a nephew of Captain Monastario, and so had to be endured.

"I do not think it a shame that Zorro might be dead," Garcia said—and quite insincerely, but he wasn't about to voice that opinion. "It is a shame that none of us were able to trap the fox ourselves and so claim the Governor's reward."

The other soldiers muttered in drunken agreement. As usual, at a time of merriment, Garcia had managed to dampen everyone's spirits. Worst of all, he was correct. The Governor's reward was substantial. The money offered for the Fox's hide was a small fortune. And the glory bestowed upon the one who beat El Zorro would be greater still.

It had been several weeks since the events of Los Rayos del Sol, where the mysterious Hidalgo de Cazador had built an enormous pyramid and enslaved hundreds by means that escaped the understanding of these soldiers. What they did know was that his purposes were sinister, and that Zorro had meted out justice.

After the incident, the Commandante Monastario claimed that his lancers had driven Cazador away, and that Zorro had been an accomplice of the Aztec priest. But their leader knew nothing about the cave Cazador had uncovered, using a squad of the King's soldiers to roll back an ancient seal of stone. Garcia had sworn them to secrecy regarding how the cave had been coated entirely in gold; not the actual substance, but a veneer of paint that had been an Aztec tribute to the golden light of the sun, not a repository for untold riches as Cazador had expected. When an explosion rocked the cavern, three immense stones fell, sealing it again, with Hidalgo el Cazador trapped behind it. The cave of fool's gold had become a fitting crypt to the false Aztec priest. In the aftermath, the soldiers had not even needed to formally disband the mission. Bereft of a leader, his bizarre hold on them broken, the peasants and Indians drifted away of their own accord, back to their previous lives. Few, it was discovered, remembered much of their time at the mission. The effects remained—bruises, cuts, emaciation, exhaustion—but even these had healed. Soon, Los Rayos del Sol was but a nightmare forgotten upon awakening to a bright dawn.

But a mystery remained. Zorro had not only escaped, he had not shown his masked face since. A rumor circulated that, having been seriously wounded in his battle with Cazador, Zorro went into hiding to heal—or, as the rumor flourished, to die. Even if the man behind the mask had not perished, it was now thought he had sufficient injuries that Zorro himself was indeed dead.

Still, many others resisted the notion. Zorro was no mere man, after all. He was not merely *named* after the fox, he possessed the spirit of the fox. It was a native belief, to be sure; but no one who had faced Zorro completely discounted the possibility that he was more than human. It seemed the only explanation for his prowess with a sword or a whip—even the brightness of his smile burned with a confidence tempered by a supernatural fire.

Yes, this was more than a man. How else to explain the ease with which Zorro had repeatedly outwitted Commandante Monastario, Sergeant Garcia and entire groups of trained soldiers? Only someone calling upon unholy and otherworldly powers could be such a menace. Such were the thoughts that consoled each soldier as he staggered home after a night in the cantina.

Lately, such weak rationalizations had been unnecessary. Despite the certainty of the Zorro's dark powers (for it could be the only explanation for their constant inability to capture him), he had appeared no more to plague them. Gatherings in the cantina once again became nightly festivals instead of occasions to debate the what-ifs of their latest encounter with, and humiliation by, The Fox. This made them joyful—on the one hand. On the other, there was unspoken agreement with Sergeant Garcia: It was a shame no one had claimed the Governor's reward.

"Yes," Gutierrez agreed in a loud voice meant to silence all other conversation in the room. Unfolding himself from the table, standing again, he resumed the role in which he was most comfortable: the center of attention. "It *is* a shame. Especially for me, since that reward would have been mine."

A snort of ridicule came from somewhere in the crowd. Gutierrez was on the man in a moment, his sword drawn and held at the surprised soldier's throat.

"You laugh? I would carve something much more intricate than a Z in your face!"

The other soldiers had judiciously controlled their reactions, despite their drunken state. To a man, they shared Sergeant Garcia's opinion of their fellow lancer. Gutierrez had boasted of his prowess with a sword since his arrival, and of the likelihood that he would be the one to finally bring Zorro to his knees. But the events at Los Rayos del Sol had occured before he had come to Los Angeles, so it appeared unlikely that he would need to support his claims. This did nothing to silence his boasts. If anything, they grew louder as they became emptier, as if amplified by the hollowness of his words. Those who scoffed at him to his face found Gutierrez quick to anger—and quick to use his sword, as well.

"Please, please." Garcia rose from the table, his fleeting philosophical mood evaporated. "We are celebrating. Save your sword for the forces that would rise against us, not those who raise a glass among us."

Gutierrez glowered at the trembling soldier for a moment longer, then lowered his sword. A broad smile broke across his face, erasing his murderous expression instantly. Even so, the other lancers could see the contempt lurking behind the innocuous grin, ready to surface at the slightest provocation.

"You are right, Sergeant Garcia," said Gutierrez. Sheathing his sword, he raised his bottle and leapt to the tabletop once more. "Another toast! May we raise the temperatures of our women's blood as high and as often as we raise our glasses!"

"Not with this much alcohol in us!" someone yelled, and the cantina shook with laughter, the tension broken.

Just then, the front door creaked open. A cool breeze stirred the fetid cantina air.

Everyone turned, startled. Laughter ceased. Hands reached unconsciously to gun handles and sword pommels. Only Zorro was apt to make an unexpected appearance at a late hour such as this. But instead of their scourge, a powerfully built man filled the doorway, gasping for breath. Through the dim haze of the cantina, the soldiers could just make out the frayed edges of the tattered clothing he wore. The man took one step forward, then fell to the ground as if doing so had been the final act of his life. Dust billowed up around his body as it hit the cantina floor.

"*Que—?*" Garcia muttered to himself. He again tried to rise from the bench in which he had comfortably settled. The effort tired him, so he sat once more. He pointed to two young soldiers. "Peréz, Manuel! Go see about that man!"

The two lancers went to the door. Private Peréz peered outside while Private Manuel knelt by the inert form on the floor.

"There's a sickly looking *burro* out here," called Peréz.

Kneeling by the body, Manuel felt for a pulse. "*Él no está muerto*, Sergeant. He is alive."

"*Aquí*," Garcia commanded. "Bring him here!"

At Garcia's command, Manuel and Peréz hoisted the stranger, grunting as they tried to support the huge man's weight on their comparably frail shoulders. Worn boots scraped the hard-packed floor as the soldiers dragged the unconscious man towards Garcia.

As they neared, Garcia noticed that the stranger wore a threadbare uniform that may have been a deep blue color in earlier days. The color now resembled that of a summer raincloud. A fur cap covering a full shock of white hair and a thick grey beard completed the image of a man who could have been a general in some ragtag army.

In the final arduous steps before the soldiers would be rid of their burden, the stranger's eyes began to flutter open. Panic lit them at the sight of a room full of armed soldiers. His head jerked from left to right at Peréz and Manuel. With a sudden shout, the stranger's arms contracted, pulling the two young soldiers together. Their heads connected with a hollow crack, instantly rendering them unconscious. They fell to the ground as limply as the stranger had done moments before. Then, quick as a cobra, the stranger seized a sword from one of the fallen soldiers and brandished it wildly.

The lancers at the table stared dumbly from their tequila-induced haze. But Gutierrez, always eager for a fight, leapt from the table and landed with his sword drawn.

"You're no Zorro, *hombre*, but you'll do just the same," he declared.

The stranger, a feral look still in his eyes, advanced upon Gutierrez. Swords clashed, the stranger just barely able to deflect a slash to his shoulder. Gutierrez pressed the stranger backwards with a series of quick jabs, each flawlessly parried. The other soldiers rose to help Gutierrez but he warned them away.

"Stay back. He is mine."

Snarling, the stranger launched an attack, slashing the lancer's left arm.

"Damn you!" Gutierrez cried, trying to ignore the pain, the blood—and, above all, the embarrassment of having been wounded before the others.

The lancer's cry of pain seemed to awaken the

stranger, as if he had been sleepwalking. For a moment, he didn't seem to know where he was, appearing not to even recognize that the object he held in his hand was a sword. The feral expression melted away in his confusion. Then the stranger noticed Gutierrez's wound and the blood soaking into the frayed cloth of the uniform. Confusion gave way to sudden understanding—he seemed to replay the events of the past few moments in his mind with growing horror.

"*Nyet!*" the stranger cried, the same strange word he had yelled before his attack. But this time, he raised his sword in one fluid motion and threw it straight up. The point embedded itself into a wood beam overhead. Quickly he dropped to his knees and bowed his head, mumbling to himself.

A humiliated Gutierrez prepared to take advantage of his opponent's defenselessness and drew back his sword. He meant to run the stranger through.

"Stop, soldier!" cried Garcia. "He is disarmed and no longer poses a threat."

Gutierrez froze, but his form seemed to stretch forward, so great was his desire to kill the man who had wounded—worse, embarrassed—him. But in the end, and as abruptly as before, he capped his emotions.

The stranger looked up, tears and weariness in his eyes.

"See to the fallen lancers," ordered Garcia. Already the two young soldiers were starting to stir. Low moans came from Peréz and Manuel as others tended to them. The red marks on their foreheads promised livid bruises. Otherwise, the pair seemed uninjured.

"Chico, Rodrigo, take charge of the man." The two designated soldiers hesitated a moment. They had seen what the stranger had done to their friends. "*Andale!*" Garcia ordered. Bracing themselves, they seized the stranger, who now made no attempt to resist.

Garcia lifted himself for what he dearly hoped would be the last time of the evening and approached the stranger, addressing him angrily.

"What do you have to say for yourself?"

"Water," said the stranger in an unfamiliar accent.

Garcia frowned. "You attack my men and ask for water? *Está loco? Hablame ahora!*"

The stranger seemed to struggle with words, then simply shrugged. "Water," he repeated sadly.

"Then you leave me no choice." Garcia signaled to Rodrigo and Chico. "*Vamos,* to the jail."

"Wait!" Gutierrez said suddenly, eyes glowing with evil mischief. He then turned to the barkeep, a man whose girth rivaled that of Garcia himself. "A bottle of vodka, Valenzuela."

"Private Gutierrez!" snapped Garcia. "What is the meaning of this?"

"*Un momento,* Sergeant," begged Gutierrez as took the bottle from Valenzuela. Then he stepped before the stranger. "This is what you really want, isn't it, *Russian*?" Gutierrez sneered.

"Private . . ." warned Garcia.

"He's a spy, Sergeant," the soldier interrupted, shaking his head at the stranger as if he were scolding a naughty boy. "And poor one at that. That word, *nyet.* It is Russian for 'río'. "

Thrusting the bottle at the man kneeling on the floor, the lancer shouted, "*This* is water to a Russian!" The stranger peered back, unintimidated, and refused to take the vodka.

"Gutierrez, don't make me ask you again!" Garcia could tell another confrontation was brewing. Still, he thought he had seen Gutierrez blanch slightly when his eyes met those of the stranger. Now the lancer seemed relieved to have an excuse to look away.

"You needn't ask. I will tell you." Gutierrez addressed the soldiers with the air of a university professor. "Do you know the reason we are all in California right now? Because the King of Spain didn't want this land to be taken over by the Russians. And surely you've heard the rumors that the Indians will be recruited into our army in case the Russians, who still hold this land dear, decide to invade."

Garcia sighed. "Surely you aren't suggesting that this man is a Russian spy?"

"I do more than suggest, I will prove. His uniform, for one."

The sergeant looked again at the stranger's tattered clothing and laughed. "Ha! If he *was* a soldier, he was discharged years ago!"

Gutierrez was not dissuaded. "A clever ruse! Only a spy would hide in plain sight that way. But he gave himself away. You all saw him fight. Only someone with fresh military training could have gained such an advantage on me."

This time, even Garcia considered the possibility. The stranger was obviously an experienced fighter, but . . .

"Another invader!" Gutierrez spat out, interrupting Garcia's train of thought.

"Like Cazador!" one lancer called out angrily.

"That's right," agreed Gutierrez. "Like Cazador—the thief!" More voices joined the chorus of indignation.

Garcia didn't like the sound of this. Gutierrez's poison had seeped into the blood of the other soldiers. And where there was poison, death often followed.

"Now, men," he began, but could not sound authoritative enough for the other soldiers, who ignored him.

"We should send this spy back to Russia in a box,"

Gutierrez declared to the incited lancers. "Maybe then, Russia will know to stay away from California."

"*Sí*," shouted the soldiers in unison.

"Let's give him the water he really wants. Hold him tight!" Chico and Rodrigo, inflamed by Gutierrez's words, tightened their grip on the stranger and forced him to his knees.

"Gutierrez—" Again, Garcia was ignored.

The stranger searched Gutierrez's face. Whatever mercy he hoped to find eluded him. He soon looked away with great resignation. The obvious danger did nothing to resurrect the feral rage from earlier. He appeared ready to accept what fate—in the form of Private Gutierrez—would decree.

Gutierrez uncapped the bottle of vodka and tipped it to the stranger's mouth.

"Drink this, spy! Drink your Russian water!"

The vodka began pouring out even before the bottle touched the stranger's lips. Clear liquid splashed on his face and stung his eyes. Gutierrez forced the bottle on the stranger, who gagged and choked on the alcohol gushing from it.

The soldiers were cheering Gutierrez on now. Sergeant Garcia may as well have been a gnat, given how the others heeded his admonitions to stop.

"Another bottle, barkeep," Gutierrez called out. "This one's almost empty."

Valenzuela—tallying in his head the bill he would send to the military—threw a full bottle to one soldier, who then tossed it to Gutierrez. The stranger was choking and sputtering, vodka soaking his beard and running down his chest.

"That's no way to treat a guest." A new voice joined the chorus, drifting down from the ceiling as if an angel had addressed the group. But the familiar voice belonged to no angel to the soldiers, except perhaps the avenging kind.

"Up in the rafters!" one lancer yelled, pointing. Their eyes searched an area of shadows the weak torchlight could not penetrate. A shape seemed crouched above them, ready to pounce like a black panther.

The voice announced the obvious: "El Zorro has returned."

With that, pistols fired into the darkness, flashes of ignited gunpowder strobing the ceiling. Revealing an empty space above them.

From behind them came the sounds of a swift series of blows. Four soldiers dropped to the floor.

"*Ay!*" cried Garcia, turning. "The scoundrel fox has tricked us again." His outrage masked his relief that Zorro was alive. After all, who would really protect them from strange invaders such as Hidalgo el Cazador? Gutierrez? Not likely.

There, amid a pile of unconscious lancers, stood a man clad entirely in black. A dark cloak billowed about him. A familiar mask partially obscured his face, but it was the roguish smile that told them all that Zorro had indeed returned from the dead. The stranger gazed up in wonder from his place on the floor.

"Liquor is for drowning sorrows, not other people." Zorro held a sword in one hand, a pistol in the other. Some of the soldiers glanced uneasily over their shoulders at the dark spot in the ceiling. They were certain the ghostly voice had emanated from there. "I am disappointed in you, Sergeant Garcia. Allowing your men to bully a weary traveler."

"But . . . but . . ." Garcia sputtered, "he attacked my men."

"True enough, but he is clearly delirious from thirst," Zorro told him. "Perhaps in his daze he was reminded of someone he didn't like very much." He addressed this last statement to Gutierrez.

"We were just lamenting your passing, Zorro." Gutierrez replied, making a great effort to appear brave. The object of his boasts before him, the lancer knew he would have to attempt to prove himself, or suffer a greater shame than having been wounded by the Russian. "Put down the gun and fight me fairly so that we may mourn your passing properly—with you truly passed on."

"Yes, I could use the sword practice." Zorro cheerily accepted what he obviously considered a minimal challenge. But first, he quickly sheathed his sword and extended his hand to the stranger, who remained staring up silently. "Stand, my friend." Once the man was on his feet, Zorro again drew his sword and attempted to hand his pistol to the stranger. "Train this on the other soldiers. Fire at them if they interfere."

The stranger seemed to understand but refused the flintlock.

"Fear not, *cabrón*," Gutierrez assured the masked man. "The others won't move. It will just be the two of us."

Zorro considered for a moment, then tucked the gun in his belt. "I accept. *En garde!*"

Gutierrez advanced toward Zorro. Their swords clashed and locked. Zorro's grin reflected no strain in holding the larger man back. After a moment, he pushed the lancer, throwing him off balance.

"Please sir," Zorro admonished, "I would have hoped my return would be met with a more earnest effort."

"Oh, I'll give you effort!" Gutierrez advanced, slashing left and right, but his long limbs moved more slowly than Zorro's and each blow was easily parried.

"Enough of an effort to make one work up a thirst

I'll grant," Zorro shrugged. As he defended himself, he manuevered himself to the bar in an almost leisurely fashion and was soon backed against the bar. Valenzuela, a great bear of a man, cowered behind the bar like a cub.

"A cup of water, barkeep," Zorro asked coolly, as if ordering a drink during a swordfight was perfectly normal. The barkeep rose from behind the bar and hesitated. "Fill it to the brim!" Zorro urged, not looking back. He was automatically defending himself against blow after blow from Gutierrez. His smile had not wavered a bit. Finally, Valenzuela complied, filling a cup with fresh water and holding it out. Zorro reached back with his free hand as the other continued to foil Gutierrez's ineffectual thrusts. Beads of sweat threatened to sting the lancer's eyes and his chest heaved with the exertion of maintaining the attack. The masked avenger, on the other hand, looked as fresh as he had upon entering the cantina. Then he was on the move again, sword dancing in one hand, cup of water in the other. Soon, he had returned to the stranger and passed him the cup. Not a drop had been spilled. "I didn't say you'd caused me to work up a thirst," Zorro laughed.

"You mock me!" Gutierrez roared and lunged. Zorro deftly stepped to the right.

"Then your mind is quicker than your blade after all!" laughed Zorro as Gutierrez's momentum threw him past his right shoulder.

But Zorro had miscalculated. The stranger stood directly in the path of Gutierrez's sword and would be run through before Zorro could react. But the stranger's animal quickness returned and in one movement, he too stepped aside as he took one last draw on the tin cup, then used it to deflect Gutierrez's sword. As he flew by, the stranger tripped him, sending the tall lancer crashing to the floor like a fallen oak.

"So!" yelled Garcia suddenly from behind Zorro. He turned on his heels toward the voice. Garcia had risen, flanked by the remaining soldiers, all with swords drawn. "You have beaten one inexperienced soldier. Let us see you how fare against a group of us at the same time!"

Knowing these drunken wretches would stand no chance against him, Zorro decided to bring this confrontation to a close.

"Against a group of inexperienced soldiers? I've always fared quite well, thank you." Zorro took one quick step forward as if to attack. As expected, even though the odds were clearly in their favor, the soldiers shrank back in fear. Instead of striking out with his sword, however, the masked man sheathed it quickly and reached both hands into his pockets. Withdrawing them a moment later, dazzling flashes of light burst from Zorro's outstretched hands. While purple dots swarmed the soldiers' vision, Zorro turned to escape.

Gutierrez, however, had risen from the floor and blocked the masked avenger's route. Zorro's own cape had shielded the lancer from the blinding flash.

"You'll have to step over my dead body to leave, Zorro," challenged the lancer shakily. The soldier was trembling with fear and excitement. He was in no condition to fight, but seemed doggedly determined to recover from the humiliations heaped upon him this night. Perhaps one more humiliation, Zorro thought, and this man will know in the future when it is better to leave well enough alone.

"A gentlemanly offer, sir, but wholly unnecessary." In a flash, Zorro retrieved his sword from its sheath and knocked Gutierrez's blade to the floor. Before the lancer could move, Zorro slashed his palm: once to the left, then diagonally down to the right, then across to the left once more.

Gutierrez cried out more from shame than the slight, stinging pain—he'd now been cut twice in one night.

Still, Zorro was not finished with the brash youth. Adding to the insult, the masked avenger used the point of his sword to prick Gutierrez in the center of his broad forehead. It was hardly enough to draw blood, but it stung awfully. Gutierrez slapped his injured hand over his face as if swatting a bee. Upon removing it, the reverse image of the Z on Gutierrez's hand appeared stamped in blood on his forehead—the mark of Zorro.

Gutierrez howled at his reflection in the mirror behind the bar and shrank away. The other soldiers were recovering from the temporary blindness. Zorro had only moments.

"Sergeant Garcia. You have always struck me as a man of some understanding that is unappreciated by your fellows."

So rarely was a compliment directed at Garcia, especially by a person of such stature as Zorro, that the Sergeant immediately began to blush with pride. He was about to reply his thanks when he saw the eyes of his men upon him. To act like a giddy schoolgirl before a known villain would undermine what little authority he wielded over his men. With a growl, he transformed the red in his face into a flash of anger.

"When these dots clear, bandit, I'll have you dancing on the end of my sword."

"And with an underappreciated sense of humor, too." Zorro smirked at the Sergeant's false bravado. "I am certain you realize that this man is but a stranger here. He is obviously exhausted and thirsty and his actions were born of a clouded mind, not a criminal desire. Please see that he is given more water, and perhaps some food. And that he is pointed in the direction of a mission, not your jail. Do that and I'm sure he will come back and apologize with all due humility."

"But my men—"

"—Will survive," Zorro insisted. "As a man of honor, please see to it." Zorro turned to Gutierrez, who now looked like an oversized baby, curled into a ball on the cantina floor. "And you, brash one. Be assured of a return visit if I find any harm has befallen our friend here." Zorro winked at Garcia. "If *you* can't keep him under control, Sergeant, insist that his uncle Monastario grasp the reins more tightly."

Zorro gave a short, formal bow to the stranger.

"Welcome, my friend."

Then Zorro was gone, melting into the night with a flourish of his ebony cloak.

Chapter 2

Don Alejandro awoke from a dream.

In the dream, father and son rode side by side, surveying the family lands. The son—*his* son, Diego de la Vega—took an interest in his family's legacy. Thoughtful questions were asked about animal husbandry. Never before glimpsed signs of responsibility surfaced. Important issues of the estate's operations were considered and frankly discussed. Days would end after long rides, father and son side by side as never before.

A magnificent dream. Opulent.

Then the reality. Screens.

The dream had been real enough in the past weeks. As if guided by some grave revelation, Diego had turned his thoughts away from his books, his aimless wandering and his flights of fancy. Apathy towards the here and now of the de la Vega estate transformed into genuine interest. Diego became more than his son. He had become Alejandro's heir.

Now screens stood between them.

"So you see, father," Diego was saying, "these Japanese screens were not only decorative, and functional as they let one dress in privacy, but they told stories as well."

Diego and Alejandro stood in the salon of the *hacienda*. The sun outside shone brightly, but its heat was tempered by a cool ocean breeze. A perfect day to ride out and inspect the land, Alejandro thought dourly.

This screen, along with several other artifacts—tapestries, clothing, additional *objets d'art*—had arrived the previous night on a ship traveling from the Orient. A wagon delivered the shipment to the de la Vega *hacienda*, just as Alejandro and Diego were about to leave on a morning inspection of the livestock.

The sight of the delicate screens made of rice paper and bamboo shattered the dream of the last several weeks.

Diego pointed to the first panel of the screen, depicting a Japanese woman whose hair was drawn up with a bow. Her face was rendered in a highly stylized manner and she wore a robe Diego had called a kimono.

"This is very simple, but each panel is a chapter in the story of this woman and the love she lost."

Alejando wrinkled his nose. "All this in three panels? Three chapters? It must be a very simple story indeed."

Diego laughed kindly and patted his father on the back. "What a shame you weren't able to join me in the education you provided. Think of how close we could be!"

Closer perhaps, Alejandro thought. But surrounded by acres of neglected land. Alejandro held his tongue.

"Actually, it is of Japan and the Orient that I have learned the least. Their culture is so different from ours or the Europeans'," Diego swept a hand across the screen. "Their way of storytelling, at least in the case of these screens, was less literal and more symbolic. This willow tree, her sadness. Her posture, hopeful. These animals, friends and family. These clouds, the potential for a good or ill resolution—for love or loss. All this in one panel."

Alejandro only saw a woman who ought to seek better shelter from the weather than a frail tree.

"This is all very interesting, I'm sure, Diego," Alejandro said gently. "But shouldn't we find out if the calf born yesterday survived? You remember the wolf tracks we found earlier in the week."

Diego shook his head, dispersing the last of Alejandro's beautiful dream. His heir had been replaced by his son—a son he loved, and dearly, but still a creature of unfulfilled promise.

"These could wait until our return," Alejandro suggested gently. "The servants could keep them safe until then."

"I couldn't think of it, father." He strode over to an open trunk and withdrew a small sculpture. "I have much to do, unpacking and arranging these treasures. It will be quite a feat to integrate these items into the Spanish decor of my bedroom. The task will require the entire day to complete, I'm sure."

Finally, Alejandro could hold his tongue no more.

"All day to decorate with trinkets and baubles from another land?" Alejandro paced the room up and down in exasperation. "No time for affairs of the *hacienda* that supports your numerous hobbies?"

Diego drew a long sigh. "I know how I must disappoint you, father. But the education you provided created a world for me, a world of art and music, science and even ideas. I revel in conundrums and tasks that challenge the mind and ignite passion. The affairs of the *hacienda* seem so far removed from that world."

"The last few weeks drew none of your usual complaints," Alejandro pointed out.

Diego nodded. "Yes, I realize I haven't been myself lately."

Alejandro nearly choked on the irony. Diego's recent attentiveness to the *hacienda*'s affairs had been most unusual, however welcome. With the arrival of these Japanese artifacts, Diego seemed to have returned to his usual maddening self.

"So these past weeks, you have been pretending?" Alejandro ceased pacing and faced his son.

"Oh no, father," Diego said quickly, "not pretending." He paused, his brow furrowing as if he were searching for the proper words. "Nor would I say that the last few weeks were a game, but they were something of . . . an experiment."

"How so?" It sounded as if his son were about to launch into another flight of fancy. Might as well listen in comfort, Alejandro thought as he wearily sank into an overstuffed chair.

"You know, of course, that this"—Diego raised his right hand—"is my dominant hand. That is, I write, throw dice, eat and drink, bow and the like with my right hand." His right hand flourished again, as it had presenting the first panel of the Japanese screen.

"Yes, of course."

"Once, I tried to change that. To make my left hand dominant. To write, eat, drink, throw dice—

everything with what had previously been my weaker hand."

"Why would one do such a thing?" A flight of most mundane fancy, Alejandro thought.

Diego just shrugged. "I don't know really. It just came to me to try. Could I change something that was fundamental to my character, such as the dominance of one hand over the other? It was quite a fascinating process of discovery."

"And did it work?"

"Not at all," Diego laughed. "My writing was unreadable, I nearly starved when all the food fell off my shaking fork, and I lost every dice game!" Even Alejandro could appreciate the humor in this and smiled. "And so it was with the affairs of the *hacienda*. I simply decided to see what it was like to be conscientious. You will be disappointed to know that it didn't suit me one bit."

Alejandro found having his golden-hued dream rendered in stark black and white very painful.

"I thought it went rather well, myself." Don Alejandro de la Vega mumbled under the weight of his disappointment.

Diego's smile flickered only for a moment before he laughed again and knelt before the chair in which his father sat.

"I speak only of the responsibilities of the *hacienda*, not of the time spent with you, father. Each moment will be cherished, of course." This lightened Alejandro's heart somewhat. "Would that we could spend such time in other pursuits." Diego stood suddenly, jabbing a finger in the air with a sudden burst of enthusiasm. In his excitement, he paced the room like his father had done minutes before. "I've got it. Let's travel together. To Japan. Come with me, we'll learn these things together. You may benefit finally from the education you provided me."

"Tempting, Diego, but who would take responsibility for the servants, the cattle, the land?" Alejandro stood to block his son from pacing further.

"Surely—"

"There is no one but me, Diego," Alejandro interrupted firmly, grasping his shoulders. "It's what I have been trying to impress upon you, young man. After me, there is only you. And if not you, no one."

This sapped all of Diego's enthusiasm. Alejandro released his son, shook his head sadly, and left the salon.

After his father left, Diego let out a sigh that would have rivaled one from Sergeant Garcia. This charade with his father was becoming more and more difficult, especially in light of the last few weeks. At least Diego had told his father part of the truth, if not the whole truth. He had indeed tested his ability to change something fundamental to his character.

Zorro's encounter with Cazador had injured him worse than anyone could have suspected. The effects of the Aztec's attack had left him with greatly reduced mobility and thrown off the coordination of his limbs. It was almost as if Cazador's paralyzing grasp continued to reach from beyond the grave. Simply holding a sword or mounting Tornado became a nearly insurmountable task. This hardly impacted the relatively sedate life of Diego de la Vega, but to Zorro the injuries were devastating. Briefly, he had despaired that perhaps the masked rider could no longer be able to fulfill his duty toward the helpless citizens of the pueblo. He himself had become helpless.

Bernardo had assured Diego that recovery was assured—as long as he took care not to overexert himself. In short, Zorro would need to lie low for a period of time. The notion seemed ludicrous, absurd—and impossible to endure. But in the end, Diego had no choice: a weakened Zorro would easily fall prey to a band of even Garcia's men. Captured and unmasked, it would destroy everything he worked for—and worse still, destroy his father. So Diego resigned himself to convalescence and directed his energies and attentions to the *hacienda*.

His father's delight in Diego's newfound interest in the *hacienda's* operations had been priceless. Of the business practices themselves, Diego actually had little to learn; he had always paid attention to these matters and had only pretended to take them for granted.

Days soon became an endless parade of mundane tasks and details. He and his father would survey their lands, count cattle, supervise employees, and— Diego's least favorite activity—examine row upon row of ledger entries to ensure the *hacienda's* finances were in order. Soon, even his father's pride failed to motivate Diego as he forced himself to remain true to his goal of applying himself as expected.

Nights in the *pueblo* did nothing to alleviate the tedium. Instead of prowling the roofs as Zorro, Diego lurked in the shadows at various social functions attended by other young, well-to-do sons and daughters of the *pueblo's* elite. The *señoritas*, he found with little surprise, were trifles, simply products their parents had been preparing all their life to "sell off" to an available bachelor when they came of age. The other *caballeros* were shallow and directionless; it was no wonder that his father worried so much about his son's future well-being. Diego found himself profoundly bored by the company of his so-called peers.

Then came the stories of those who suspected that Zorro had been killed. As the idea gained acceptance, things in the *pueblo* began to change again. The military and others started to lose their fear of reprisals for acts of oppression against Indians and any other powerless unfortunates who crossed their paths. These were minor injustices at first. But with each one to which Zorro failed to respond, the seriousness of the offenses grew.

Finally, Diego had healed well enough to don his second skin, the mask and cape of El Zorro. At first, he rode Tornado fast and hard into the desert. The stallion's churning muscles reminded him of the action on which Zorro had thrived. The coolness of the crisp, dry air invigorated his body and rejuvenated his spirit. The scent of sweet desert wildflowers, of the pungent mariposa lily and delicate fairy duster, excited his dulled senses.

Diego inhaled deeply, the desert perfume still lingering, the sensations recalled from the night before charging even the austere atmosphere of the salon. He raised his hands before him, closing them around nothing, but feeling the cool grip of his sword, even exulting in his memory of how the weight of the barbaric gun had felt in his grasp. This after so much time.

Examining his hands more closely, Diego remembered another partial truth he had told his father. He had indeed attempted to become left-handed even though he had grown up right-handed. The result was not failure, as he had stated earlier; Diego had become ambidextrous. He found he could no longer favor one side or the other exclusively. And so it was with Diego and Zorro—one required the other for balance. Anything less would be to deny a fundamental part of him.

Looking up, he saw the family servant, Bernardo, waiting respectfully at the salon's entrance, not having wanted to interrupt his young master's reverie. Smiling as their eyes met, Bernardo led in a small group of his own assistants, using sign language to designate the Japanese treasures to be taken from the room. Efficient in his duties as head of the household staff, Bernardo was much more than just a family servant. He was also the faithful friend, confidant, assistant, and teacher of Zorro. The only living person aware of Diego's dual identity, he served as an extra pair of eyes in the *pueblo* among the common citizenry. His demeanor, usually impervious to shock or surprise, lent credence to the mistaken belief that because he was a mute, he was also deaf. As a result, many a whispered rumor, secret, or innuendo passing between conspirators was often intercepted by Bernardo, whom they thought unable to hear. However, it was the loyalty and friendship born of years of shared experience that made Bernardo a vital part of Diego's life.

For now, Bernardo played the dutiful servant, and soon the room was nearly empty. Despite his usual stoicism, Diego's beloved friend eyed the one remaining crate that had not yet been pried open with some amount of excitement.

"Yes, old friend," Diego laughed. "The ship brought more than rice-paper screens and books of haiku."

Self-consciously, Bernardo instantly masked his excitement, which amused Diego even more. The arrival of exotic items to study, catalogue, and experiment with always animated Bernardo's usually impassive demeanor, no matter how hard he tried to contain it.

"I suspect the vessel was carrying at least one passenger of interest, as well."

Bernardo instantly looked up from the mysterious crate, his expression one of concern. Holding his fingers to his lips so that Diego would pause in his story, the servant walked to the door leading into the salon, checked to ensure they were alone, then shut it. Satisfied no one could overhear, Bernardo nodded for Diego to continue. He recounted the Russian's arrival and the subsequent encounter with the lancers at the cantina.

"We must make discreet inquiries at the mission to which the Russian was going that night. I must ensure he continues to be treated as Zorro instructed. Further, I sense the man is more than just a poor immigrant."

Bernardo looked at him sharply.

"No, Bernardo, I don't think he's a spy, as Guiterrez charged. As we know, that man is a fool. But the Russian did have on clothes that in better days may have been a uniform. And his reflexes were uncanny." Diego remembered the speed with which the Russian had deflected Guiterrez's charge with only a tin cup.

"Meanwhile," Diego continued, "the flashpaper you prepared performed splendidly. The lancers were certain I had conjured flames from my hands."

Bernardo was pleased at the success of the flashpaper. It had been another trick borrowed from the magicians Diego so admired. He had coated very thin paper with gunpowder. Zorro had stored these in his pockets along with a flint from which to make a spark. When he had reached into his pockets, he had held a sheet of coated paper in each hand, along with a small piece of flint. Diego had practiced striking the flint to create a spark as he withdrew his hands, igniting the papers. They burned instantly and completely, producing the flash that had dazzled Garcia and his men.

Diego gestured to the still unopened crate before them, then stooped to lift it. "Let's see what other surprises we'll have in store for the lancers."

Excitement once again lit Bernardo's face as he crossed the salon to the large, ornate marble fireplace. Its mantle rose up to nearly his height. A man could easily stand within the hearth with only the top of his head entering the flue. Diego himself had designed the fireplace, and his father had always found it ostentatious even for his own tastes. But of course, its design was much more functional than his father could appreciate.

Bernardo lifted his hand to one column carved from pink marble. The stone felt smooth and cool to the touch—it had been months since the last fire had crackled in its hearth. Sweeping his hand down, probing the grooves with his fingertips, he seemed to be simply admiring the craftsmanship. Instead, the gesture triggered a mechanism that produced an audible click. A seam appeared in the cinderblocks on the back wall of the fireplace. Then they slid apart entirely.

Bernardo stepped into the fireplace, now the entrance to a subterranean passageway. And a secret entrance to Zorro's lair. Diego followed closely behind. As soon as they were both in the passageway, the cinderblocks slid closed once more, plunging them instantly into darkness. This lasted only moments as a torch blossomed, ignited by Bernardo. Its light revealed a sloping tunnel down which they traveled.

A short distance away they arrived at a ledge above what appeared to be a great pit in the earth. Bernardo touched the flame of his torch to a lantern set in the stone wall. Before them, a wooden staircase descended into the murky blackness. As they walked down the stairs, Bernardo paused every ten feet to light another lantern, each seeming to summon the next several steps out of the darkness. After the sixth wall-mounted lantern, the staircase ended at a stone floor. By now, firelight had transformed the murky pit into a great chamber, stalactites lining the vaulted ceiling as if the men stood in the maw of some immense, ancient beast.

Diego set the crate on a nearby table while Bernardo lit the remaining lanterns that ringed the chamber. Each new flame revealed an additional detail of the lair—the alcove containing the grindstone upon which Bernardo diligently sharpened Zorro's blade; dusty trunks and shelves filled with even dustier books containing both the latest and the most ancient information that Zorro could make use of in his quest for justice; their "science" table, heaped with equipment collected from all over the world, most purchased at great expense: a microscope, sextants, various chemical compounds, schematics for fantastic machines such as submarines and hot air balloons, as well as plans for other devices with applications they had not yet divined.

Bernardo rejoined Diego at the table, a crowbar now in his hand. As they regarded the crate like acolytes before a sacred relic, the faithful servant offered the crowbar to Diego. He refused it with a smile.

"I wouldn't think of depriving you of the honor," he told Bernardo. Though he had been trying to conceal his excitement, Diego could tell his friend was nearly beside himself with curiosity about what the crate held. "You act like a child who has broken the *piñata* at his own birthday fiesta, my friend!"

This time, Bernardo returned the smile unabash-
edly, and after several quick, splintering cracks, tore
the lid from the crate. Together, the pair pulled out
the packing fibers. The treasures were finally revealed.
Bernardo reached in and withdrew a scroll of delicate
rice paper. Untying the silk ribbon that bound the
document, he unrolled it on the table. The scroll was
painted with indecipherable Japanese characters beside which were drawn diagrams of various weapons.
A packing list, Diego realized. One he had no hope
of reading. Instead, he reached into the box and withdrew an object made of sturdier material, relying
upon his scant knowledge of Japanese weaponry to
assist his identification of the crate's contents.

The item he held was only two inches in diameter,
made of metal and shaped like a snowflake. A deadly
snowflake, Diego thought as he took the object carefully. Each point had been sharpened to a razor's
edge.

"Not a snowflake," Diego said out loud, searching
his memory. "A star. Correct Bernardo?" The servant
nodded. "*Shuriken*. A throwing star."

Next, Diego withdrew a set of weapons that resembled spearheads with handles. Turning one in his
hand, he was impressed by the comfort of its leather-
bound grip. Its balance and heft made it perfect for
throwing. "*Kunai*," he said, plucking the name from
the memory of a book read in the distant past. "A
versatile weapon, useful as a knife, shovel, even ham-
mer; and, of course, a throwing dagger."

Bernardo held a *kunai* as well, scrutinizing each
detail of its construction.

The crate contained even more items, some iden-
tifiable—two small clubs joined by a short chain,
known as *nunchuks*—and others of which Diego or

Bernardo possessed no knowledge. One box within the crate held a number of small, four-pointed metal barbs, each able to fit comfortably in a man's palm—that is, if a man found pleasure in gripping sharp implements. Two other items retrieved from the crate appeared to be brother and sister weapons. Each was comprised of a long chain that ended in either a small sickle or a metal ball. Deadly siblings indeed, thought Diego.

He watched Bernardo, neatly laying out the dangerous implements, the family servant's remarkable mind already racing to catalogue the items and the distinguishing features of each. He would only commit these observations to paper for Diego's benefit; no matter how minute the detail, any information, once absorbed by Bernardo's mind, was never forgotten.

"It would be quite a family that would fill a *piñata* with toys such as these, eh, old friend?" Diego said, referring to Bernardo's initial adolescent excitement over the crate's contents. Totally engrossed in his study of the weapons, he ignored Diego. This happened often, so Diego was not insulted. The child that had come out to play for a brief moment had simply left behind an adult with work to do.

Diego lifted one throwing star from the table, disturbing Bernardo's careful arrangement, and the servant looked up with annoyance. The younger man shrugged away the glance with a smile.

"Beautiful, isn't it?" Then, with a flick of his wrist, Diego flung the *shuriken* across the chamber where it bit deeply into a wooden post. He examined where the star had struck the post. "And to think it shares the same principles of form and function as the benign rice paper screen, eh, old friend?"

Chapter 3

Insomnia always struck Felipe Rosario after the most exhausting days. Today he had baked in the summer sun, breathing the dust kicked up by restless horses as he shoed them. The same sun scorched him as he cleaned the stables at the lush Rancho Marcos. Straw remained clinging his body, the reek of manure rising from him in waves.

The sun had sunk boiling into the ocean hours ago, and Felipe now lay on his back in front of his adobe hut, part of a small cluster of peasant homes developing just north of the *pueblo*. He stared up at the heavens, contemplating the stars that clustered together as glowing clouds. His hands lay on his chest, his dry, cracked finger laced together. His breath wheezed from his lungs. Sleep was hours away, and when it came, it would take him where he lay. Maria, his wife, would find him here in the morning, as she was now accustomed to doing. Felipe's eyes would be closed, his hands still folded on his chest, and only his muted wheezing would indicate that he was alive.

The stars were souls in heaven, Felipe Rosario had been told as a child, and he continued to believe it. Tonight he saw no beauty in them. Instead, he saw the price of Spain's invasion of California. Each pinpoint of light in heaven signaled the flame of a life snuffed out here on earth. The souls of the Indians most certainly made heaven blaze brightly. First diseases brought by the invaders had decimated the native population. Then came enslavement and mistreatment, as he witnessed daily on the Marcos Ranch—as he had witnessed just today, which put him in this somber mood. He was a religious man, and believed that the natives could benefit from knowledge of the Christian God. But the missions had not shown the Indians the gates of heaven so much as herded them through those gates at a forced march.

Felipe wheezed a deep sigh. There would be a reckoning. What he had been taught, and what little he had been able to read of the Bible, had told him this was so. Judging by the number of stars in the sky, this could come soon. Any more stars, any more souls sent to heaven, and night would disappear altogether.

He may have dozed. Later he would admit to this possibility. But at that moment, there was no passage of time between his last thought of souls and the sight of four stars detaching themselves from heaven and falling to the earth. Falling stars, fallen souls, and at the same time, a ghostly music. Thin, flutelike, with a delicate melody whose occasional dissonance was beautiful.

Felipe raised himself up on his elbows, eyes blinking, disbelieving the phenomenon.

The four twinkling stars were at the horizon and growing, ever so slowly. Along with them, the reedy music increased in volume. Felipe sat up fully. The whitish lights now burned yellow and orange. They were no longer stars, but balls of flame rushing toward him.

Still mesmerized by an event that seemed beyond his comprehension, Felipe staggered to his feet.

The sound of galloping hooves began to mingle with that of the mysterious melody. Soon it became apparent that these flames were not carried by some celestial power, but by horses. Powerful ones. Their thundering approach filled his ears and he had to bring both hands up to muffle the sound. Disoriented, Felipe stumbled into the main road leading to the *pueblo,* and stood directly in the path of the horse-drawn comets.

The music ceased.

Shortly, four horses thundered to a nervous stop in front of him. Each was pitch-black, appearing as a pair of wild eyes floating above gleaming ebony hooves. Ghost horses. And astride these beasts, four figures held burning torches aloft as if each carried the devil's standard.

The riders themselves were monsters.

These were not merely the demons of his well-worn Bible, but creatures born of some unfathomable nightmare. Each possessed a reptilian snout and fang-lined jaws. Above, black slits of eyes stared down coldly. Their skin appeared to be composed of long scales, like that of some lethal snake or lizard. One monster, who appeared to be their leader, brought its torch before its face and roared. A gout of flame rushed at Felipe. Shielding his face with his arm, Felipe screamed in terror, realizing what these creatures were: dragons. Frightened as he was, Felipe found himself unable to look away from the sight of the fire-light dancing on the dragons' leers. Smoke curled from the leader's nostrils in the aftermath of the attack.

The Dragon Rider to the leader's left glared at Felipe, its face a mask of pure evil. In contrast, the rider to the right possessed a ghoulish smile, yet it seemed no less malevolent. Exaggerated fangs, like those of a prehistoric cat, and a feathered mane distinguished the final rider.

The leader pointed a claw at Felipe. The ranch hand wailed and sank to his knees. He was awake now. So, too, were others.

Felipe could hear a commotion rising behind him. The thundering arrival of the riders, followed by the ranch hand's cries of terror, had roused several in the tiny village. Shouts of confusion, fear, and anger rose from the surrounding adobe huts. Men hastily pulled on clothes and looked toward the bizarre scene of the small man kneeling as if in prayer before the four figures on horseback.

The leader barked a command in some alien tongue and pointed again. This time, his target was the village itself. Two of the riders spurred their horses and plunged into the heart of the town, knocking Felipe aside and nearly crushing him.

Through Felipe's terror, he heard a familiar sound through the horses' galloping: a metallic scraping. Looking up, he saw a sword held aloft by the feather-maned dragon. On its highly polished surface danced orange torchlight. The effect was both beautiful and terrible at the same time. In it, Felipe saw his death. He bowed his head. Perhaps the dragon would see his supplication and bring the blade down quickly and cleanly.

"*Felipe!*"

A woman's voice floated out of the rising din behind him. Maria. He jerked his gaze away from the ground to the adobe behind him. Beyond, fire and smoke rose from the *pueblo,* but for the moment, he could only see his wife, running from their home. She must not see. She must not be harmed.

"Stay!" he cried, but she ignored him. Only steps away.

He looked up at the Dragon Rider, its arm frozen, poised to strike. It faced Felipe's wife, its features still glowing with evil and hatred. Still, the dragon did not strike. It looked down at Felipe, then back at Maria. Abruptly, the rider spurred its horse and, pulling back on the reins, caused the horse to sail directly over Felipe and off into the *pueblo.*

Just then, a panicked Maria arrived at his side. As she threw her arms around him, Felipe said a prayer. The Dragon Rider had spared him. Spared them both.

But had it?

Felipe rose from the ground in his wife's arms. She seemed not to notice the dust, the odor of manure—any of the usual aggravations. Her eyes were looking beyond him and back at the village, where shots had begun to ring out.

The dragons had not spared them, had not given him a painless death, as he had hoped. Instead, they had merely allowed him to live to bear witness the destruction of his home, and those of his neighbors. Flames, born of the Dragon Riders' torches, or perhaps their fiery breath, leapt from the roofs of many homes. As some battled the flames threatening to engulf their homes, others gathered to engage the invaders.

Meanwhile, the Dragon Riders cut a path of destruction through the little community.

The leader rode past the small general store and threw his torch through a window. The dry goods inside immediately burst into flame. The burning grains crackled in a violent staccato, filling the night as if a war had broken out. This accounted for many of the gunshots heard by Felipe and others; other gunshots, however, were quite real.

One man fired upon the dragon leader. Whether due to the dragon's thick hide, the shooter's smoke- and sleep-filled eyes, or the beast's otherworldly invincibility, the attack brought forth only anger, not blood.

The Dragon Rider turned on its would-be assassin. Crossing its arms, it reached like a gunslinger toward holsters on the opposite sides of its body. Instead of guns, however, the creature withdrew a pair of swords, one shorter than the other.

Unable to reload his gun, the peasant dropped it and attempted to retreat. However, the ghostly horse easily overtook the man. The dragon slashed out with his sword and the man fell to the ground, alive, but not likely to walk again.

In another part of the *pueblo*, the most vicious-looking dragon did his part bringing destruction to the little town. Almost magically, he would appear from between two buildings, a fire burning behind him. Then he would be gone again, only to reappear in the opposite direction from which he had been travelling. This Dragon Rider also seemed immune to the men's guns. Its speed and agility, its erratic movement, made it difficult for any to draw proper aim.

A small group of men, swords drawn, charged the monster. Even though their blood ran cold at the sight of the apparition, they drew strength in unity. The Dragon Rider merely roared at the men and met their charge.

Swords clashed, and the men were quickly disarmed in one sweep of the dragon's sword. Two men lost fingers in the attack and fell to the ground grasping their ruined hands. The Dragon Rider's horse reared suddenly, scattering those men not writhing in agony, and rode on.

Elsewhere, the laughing dragon seemed almost lackadaisical, though no less destructive. As if arriving for a friendly visit, it dismounted at a hitching post, tying up its horse. At first, the horse pawed and snorted unhappily, but the laughing dragon calmed it with a pat on the snout.

Another band of brave men prepared to drive away the Dragon Rider that dared to meet them on foot.

The laughing dragon merely surveyed them with interest, its frozen leer seeming to widen in the flickering light of burning buildings.

It walked slowly to meet them. The men ready to challenge the monster noticed the sword at its side, and a large club strapped to its back. Though clearly outnumbered, the laughing dragon made no move to arm itself.

"Kill it!" one man cried, and they rushed forward.

The dragon seemed to sink abruptly into the earth. One moment it was there, then gone. Then a bizarre yelp, like an Indian war cry, filled the air. The men turned towards the sound, but by then, the nearest defender had fallen to the ground in agony.

The dragon had rolled to the side in a blur, leapt up and kicked the man, breaking his shoulder. Landing nimbly on its feet, slightly crouched, the rider held out its clawed hands, gesturing in the air. Finding their imminent defeat amusing, it laughed evilly.

Hoping to overwhelm their foe, two men attacked at the same time. Their swords were easily deflected by the demon's scales. His hands deftly evading the blades, the dragon grasped each man by the forearm and twisted, wrenching them painfully, and threw both men to the ground. Luckily, the men had dropped their swords, or their agonized flailing would have caused themselves more injury than that which Dragon Rider had already inflicted upon them.

The laughing dragon again jumped at those who remained standing. Each man received a crushing kick to the chest and soon lay in the dust, gasping for breath.

Unerringly landing on its feet once more, the laughing dragon resumed its offensive stance. Its opponents lay in a broken heap before him, not likely to rise. The Dragon Rider nodded toward them, turned, and simply strolled away, laughing.

Suddenly, a man who had been lying hidden sprang at the Dragon Rider. Instead of catching it off guard, the dragon, barely breaking its stride, lashed out with a spinning kick, striking the man in the left cheek. Bone shattered. The force sent the man into the wall of a nearby building, down which he slumped to the ground, unconscious.

The Dragon Rider did not look back as he continued walking through the village.

The feather-maned dragon burst through a cloud of smoke astride its horse. Rather than use its sword, the torch itself became the dragon's weapon. The flames struck out at anyone foolhardy enough to cross the rider's path. More than one man was set alight.

In their panic, some served the creature's purpose and set fire to the buildings to which they ran for shelter.

Finally, a peasant drew a gun against the feathered dragon. Before the man could fire, the torch flew at the gun as if drawn to it by an elastic cord. The flame ignited the powder prematurely and the gun exploded in the man's hand. The ball fired harmlessly into the ground.

The Dragon Rider unsheathed its sword once more. Again, it was raised, poised to strike as it rode toward the man with the ruined hand.

At that moment, the leader appeared, barking out another command in its alien language. The feather-maned dragon shifted its course to meet the leader and the man sank to the dusty ground in relief. The vicious dragon joined its cohorts along with the laughing dragon. The creatures seemed to confer with each other, then turned to survey their work.

The leader nodded with satisfaction.

The completely subdued peasants could only hold their breath and await the Dragon Riders' next move.

The lead rider hissed another command and spurred his horse. The others followed suit and all four began riding out of the *pueblo*.

Felipe Rosario still stood with Maria, having witnessed the entire savage onslaught. They held each other as the monsters rode by, ignoring the pair as they did so. The poor husband and wife continued to embrace each other as they watched the Dragon Rider's retreat. Without the torches to mark their progress, the monsters were soon swallowed by the night.

Chapter 4

News of the incident caused so great an uproar that the next morning Captain Monastario felt compelled to investigate personally. As he rode the main thoroughfare on his horse, he stroked his mustache unconsciously and took in the scene.

Fire damage was widely in evidence. Smoke hung in the air, fed by the still-smoldering ruins. Frightened villagers lined the streets, looking up at the *comandante* for some guidance, some explanation. They did not like him, did not respect him, but the horror of the previous night made them realize their dependence upon him. They needed his protection from these creatures. This dependence shamed them; Monastario could see it in their pleading eyes.

Normally, he took pride in the expressions of fear, shame, even loathing that he inspired. These were signs of the power he wielded over them. Today, though, he felt slightly shamed himself. The *pueblo* appeared as though a small army had overrun it. And all while he had been indulging in a tryst that had not been entirely pleasurable. Zorro may have been Monastario's gadfly, but the perpetrators of this devastation were a swarm of angry hornets. It was a miracle, really, that no one had actually been killed. Some animals had perished, but despite the serious wounds the invaders—dubbed the Dragon Riders by the typically superstitious *pobladores*—had inflicted, they had refrained from killing anyone. And as he surveyed the ruined *pueblo*, he was certain that the horsemen could easily have killed, had they chosen to do so.

But why had they chosen such a terrifying mercy? And when would the killing begin?

A grunt from beside Monastario brought him back to himself. For once he was glad that Sergeant Garcia, who had accompanied him along with a group of lancers, was incapable of remaining silent for very long; some sound inevitably escaped from one orifice or another. While utterly repulsive, at least this time he had jolted Monastario from an unpleasant daydream.

"Does the sight of this destruction disturb you, sergeant?" snapped the *commandante*.

The gait of his horse jostling his bulk from side to side, Garcia opened his mouth to answer, but Monastario interrupted before he could speak.

"I would guess you had no stomach for such things, but your fat belly makes you seem all stomach!"

Garcia snapped his mouth shut like a larger fish gulping down a minnow. He knew it was the devastation around them that was provoking his commander, but there was no need to say the wrong thing and make it worse for himself. Luckily, a crowd of peasants had begun to gather, and Monastario would hesitate to make too much of a scene in front of them. Sure enough, the *commandante* swallowed his rage and composed himself. Clearing his throat, Monastario adopted an official tone of voice and addressed the crowd.

"As the military commander for Los Angeles, I assure you that you will be safe." Silence from the crowd. "From now on," he added. "There are no dragons or ghostly horsemen. Just ordinary bandits with extraordinary theatricals." He then turned to Garcia and the other lancers, motioning for them to follow. Without another word, and now scrupulously avoiding eye contact, Monastario led the group out of the village, just beyond the remains of Felipe Rosario's hut.

As soon as they had left the tiny community behind, Monastario stopped the group and addressed Sergeant Garcia.

"So tell me, Sergeant, what did your men discover when they followed the tracks out into the desert."

Garcia licked his lips. He thought he still tasted last night's beer on them. "Well, yes, there were indeed tracks, *commandante*."

Monastario waited expectantly. Garcia frowned. He didn't want to say what he had to say next. But he hadn't the imagination or the quickness to find another way to say it.

"My men found that the hoof tracks went deep into the desert, then simply stopped."

Monastario frowned. "What do you mean stopped?"

The sergeant opened his mouth, but Monastario interrupted again. Garcia gulped another minnow.

"You mean to suggest our dragons simply flew

away, Sergeant?" Monastario leaned into Garcia, spittle flying from the *commandante*'s mouth. This time, there was no crowd of civilians to prevent a scene. Garcia steeled himself.

"It would fit the descriptions of the culprits, sir," Garcia said reluctantly.

Monastario threw his head back to laugh, but when he looked again at Garcia, there was anything but good humor in his eyes.

"Idiot. If they were truly dragons, they would have eaten their horses, not ridden them."

"The tracks did cease, *commandante*, so perhaps—"

Monastario silenced him with a growl of exasperation. "Some bandits with festival costumes laid waste to part of a *pueblo*. Within *my* jurisdiction. And I'd like to know where your lazy ass was resting while these people were being massacred."

Garcia wanted to point out that, since no one was killed, it was technically not a massacre, but he was spared the need to respond by a new voice.

"*Commandante* Monastario. Dear Sergeant Garcia!" The voice came from Don Diego de la Vega. The young man approached, coughing slightly from the smoke-filled air.

"Don Diego," acknowledged Monastario with a terse bow and rigid smile.

"My friend!" cried Garcia. Though they were not actually friends, he truly liked the young man so he felt emboldened to greet the Don Diego with some familiarity, especially in front of his *commandante*.

"What might I do for you, sir?" Monastario said quickly. He hoped to rid himself of Don Diego as quickly as possible. "We are in the midst of an important investigation at this moment. Some very dangerous and destructive criminals are at large."

"So that is what happened in the little village," Diego said, indicating the ruined huts behind them. "And here I thought I had missed a most exciting festival."

The young man was obviously joking, but Monastario had a small suspicion it was his expense. Such subtle mockery seemed to underscore all of his conversations with the *caballero*, but the *commandante* was never absolutely certain. And it certainly would not do to make rash accusations against the son of a prominent landowner such as Alejandro de la Vega, whom he knew to be loyal to the King.

"I went out for a long ride in the fresh air," Diego explained, "and suddenly, fresh air became scarce. Should I or my father be concerned?"

"Not at all, Don Diego," said Monastario. "Some bandits caused quite a bit of trouble, but things look worse than they really are. My men arrived in time to drive them off." A small lie he hoped the young man would not notice. "Despite the damage to homes, no lives were lost."

"Excellent work, *Commandante*," Diego replied effusively. "How many bandits were there? Surely twenty or thirty? You'll need more men, I'm certain."

"Four, actually," Monastario admitted reluctantly. "But the attack came deep in the night when the citizens were sleeping, thus the extent of the damage."

"Sleeping, indeed." He scrutinized Monastario. "And may I say that you look remarkably rested for a man who must have been awakened violently and called into battle in the middle of the night. You have stamina far beyond that of my own, I can assure you." He grinned at the *commandante*, who could only smile uncomfortably back. Never had praise seemed so insulting.

"Thank you, Señor de la Vega. Now—"

"It's a wonder," Diego continued, "That a man of your obvious fortitude hasn't captured the accursed Zorro yet. The scoundrel must lead a truly charmed life to have remained at large for so long."

"Señor de la Vega," Monastario finally huffed. "Please excuse us. You'll agree these villains must be apprehended."

"At all costs," Don Diego agreed. "I apologize for being a nuisance."

"Not at all, Señor de la Vega," replied Monastario, hoping it didn't show on his face how much he *did* think Diego was a nuisance. But the younger man simply smiled blandly. Nonetheless, mockery seemed to hide just behind the innocuous expression.

With a nod to Sergeant Garcia, Don Diego finally turned his horse, which trotted away through the *pueblo*.

As soon as Don Diego's form was obscured by the smoky haze, Monastario turned to Garcia, seething with pent-up frustration.

"You will find these men and bring them in, do you hear?"

"Yes sir, *commandante*!" Garcia saluted mechanically. He had no idea where to begin the investigation.

"Forgive me, *commandante*," came a soldier's voice. Gutierrez approached on his horse. "I believe I know the ringleader of these bandits."

Monastario raised an amused eyebrow. Don Diego was instantly forgotten. Now that he had been shamed by Zorro, doubtless his nephew had found another target for his fanciful claims.

"Explain," Monastario commanded.

"The Russian," Gutierrez stated flatly. "The man who entered the tavern and was championed by Zorro. No doubt he is behind this atrocity."

"Oh?" Monastario's fingers began to smooth his mustache once more.

"He exhibited extraordinary physical skills. And spoke in a tongue no one in this poor village would recognize."

Monastario nodded the possibility of his agreement. Encouraged by a sign that his uncle was considering his theory, Gutierrez became more animated, and bolder in his statements.

"I repeat what I said then, that the man is an invader. No doubt he has come to pave the way for the Russians to attempt to take this land. I wouldn't be surprised if Zorro was part of this plot."

The moment he uttered Zorro's name, Gutierrez knew he had gone too far. His uncle's lip twitched to suppress a sneer, but he did not pounce immediately. Instead, the *commandante* remained silent a few more moments, absently twisting his pencil-thin mustache as if turning the notion over in his mind. This lasted just long enough for Gutierrez to think that perhaps he had not overreached after all.

"An interesting theory," Monastario finally said. He had not considered Gutierrez's idea in the least. The *commandante* merely took the time to observe his nephew, planning to speak when the boy's defenses had been lowered. The earnest expression in Gutierrez's face told him it was time to strike. "An interesting theory, but utterly insupportable."

Gutierrez winced at the rebuke, as Monastario had planned. As commander of the lancers as well as the private's uncle, it would probably do to be more supportive, but the boy's statements were too outrageous.

By making Gutierrez feel a fool, he hoped to teach him to stop playing the fool.

"You would link Zorro, with whom we are painfully familiar, a poor Russian peasant whom you suspect of leading an invasion, and four costumed bandits? Please enlighten me on the logic that connects these events, I appear to be missing it."

Even though Gutierrez himself did not necessarily believe Zorro was party to the Dragon Riders' raid, he ventured an explanation anyway. Knowing he was wrong had never stopped him from forging ahead before.

"Zorro's appearance after such a lengthy absence was quite fortunate for the Russian, don't you think?" He paused. His uncle was clearly unimpressed, but did not interrupt. "Perhaps Zorro has been abroad, making a deal with the Russians. At the cantina, the scoundrel was simply protecting an ally. I suggest that the incident was no coincidence. And the Dragon Riders. Who's to say they are not Zorro and the Russian, along with two comrades?" Put that way, Gutierrez thought, the logic seemed unassailable. Having convinced himself of what only moments before he had not believed, he felt confident of his uncle's support.

"Who's to say they are?" Monastario asked, destroying two theories in one blow. "I find it unlikely that Zorro would be party to an attack on the very people has been hell-bent to protect. However," he added after a dramatic pause, "this Russian might be worth investigation."

Gutierrez could hardly believe his ears. His uncle, after all, had taken something he said seriously.

Garcia spoke up. "May I point out, *commandante*,

that Zorro has given a warning about what will happen should the Russian be harmed."

"Are we to be afraid of Zorro?" Monastario snapped. "Is he your *commandante* or am I?"

While Garcia was sputtering a reply, Gutierrez jumped into the fray. Something the stupid sergeant had said gave him an idea, one he didn't want to forget while he was in his uncle's good graces.

"Zorro has put himself in an unfortunate position, Uncle," Gutierrez said quickly. "What better trap to lay for him than to arrest the Russian? The Fox will be compelled to rescue his newfound friend, only to find himself at the mercy of a squad of lancers prepared for his appearance. Finally, we will take him by surprise."

Monastario nearly pulled half of his mustache off. Now that was inspiration! Use Zorro's code of honor against him.

"Of course!" Monastario nearly shouted. He turned to the sergeant. "Garcia, see that Gutierrez is given the resources to carry out his plan. Roust the Russian, arrest him and jail him. We may catch our fox yet!"

"Yes, sir! Absolutely, sir." Then Garcia paused a moment. "And the horsemen?"

Monastario rolled his eyes. "Find them, of course, sergeant. That will be your task. Hopefully, it is simple enough to be executed even by you."

"I assure you it is, *commandante*!" Garcia answered.

Monastario frowned. "The only thing you could assure me of, sergeant, is your appetite. Carry on." Dismissing Garcia, he turned to Gutierrez.

"Bring me The Fox, soldier."

Chapter 5

Diego emerged from the opposite end of the village where he had met Monastario and Garcia. Finally, he lowered the handkerchief he had used to protect himself from the acrid smoke.

Four bandits. This fact disturbed Diego. It was a small number, and the destruction so great.

To be fair, what Monastario had said was probably accurate—except for the part concerning the soldiers that had supposedly driven away the raiders. That, Diego was certain, was a classic Monastario fabrication. Besides that, however, no doubt many of the peasants had been asleep as the attack commenced. And surely few had regained full consciousness before it was over.

As a result, four bandits decimated a *pueblo*.

While riding through the village, he had heard snatches of conversation that drifted through the *pueblo* as thickly as the smoke. The Dragon Riders. Creatures of fire and fangs and feathers. Unearthly music. No doubt it was all a kind of frightening ruse. But to what end?

Later he would send Bernardo to discreetly inquire about details. He had a knack, among his many knacks, for piercing the veil of superstition and extracting useful information from the peasants. The soldiers, with their blunt ways, wouldn't gather half the clues Bernardo could. But Diego needed only his intuition to realize that this was not an isolated incident. These "dragons" would ride again.

The attack on the village had clearly been a prelude. But to what? And why?

Diego spurred his horse, a fine Arabian from his father's stables, to a gallop on a course for the *hacienda*. Unraveling the mystery of the Dragon Riders had become a priority. Bernardo would be vital to this task. Either as Diego or as Zorro, at least until the sun went down, he would be too conspicuous in the *pueblo*; Bernardo, on the other hand, would be practically invisible.

Far from the village, the stench of smoke and destruction once again gave way to the clean, sweet smell of the desert. Diego slowed his horse to a trot, using the tranquil atmosphere to help him contemplate the matters at hand. Shortly, the rustle of a small plant ahead drew his attention. As the horse approached the spot, a small brown reptile darted across the trail. A horned toad, Diego noted as it skittered before him; a creature able to squirt blood from its eyes by breaking tiny vessels when cornered by an enemy. The surprise—and Diego doubted any creature would not be surprised at its quarry performing *that* bizarre feat—would allow the horned toad to escape. And despite its name, the creature was a lizard, not a toad at all. Overall, a very curious creature.

Diego followed the horned toad until it found shelter beneath the tangled branches of a creosote bush and disappeared. It reminded him of the Russian that Zorro had saved at the cantina. There was someone who had darted across Zorro's path. And he, too, had disappeared, Zorro recalled, thinking back on the events of two nights before. Exiting the cantina minutes after Zorro's warning to Gutierrez, the Russian had offered the tin cup to the *burro* tied outside. It drank greedily, in no better condition than its master had been. Further giving it rest, the stranger walked beside the *burro* as they headed east towards the nearest mission. Zorro, who watched from the shadows to make certain no further ill befell the visitor, followed at a discreet distance.

During that time, he had an overwhelming sensation that the Russian was aware of him. He was reminded of Cazador. While he had possessed no true mystical powers, the Aztec priest's awareness of the world around him had been almost preternatural. Zorro himself had developed powerful senses as well. But now and again, the Russian would glance his way, his gaze piercing the darkness and peeling away any plant or rock behind which The Fox hid and looked directly at Zorro. Here, too, was another extraordinary person.

That much had been obvious in the cantina. His blinding speed. His skills with a sword. His strength.

Earlier the next day, Bernardo had made the inquiries that Diego had instructed and he found that the Russian had never arrived at the Mission. The *padres* had taken in no strangers. The Russian had simply vanished. Impossible, of course, but his whereabouts were presently unknown. Diego's ride that morning had been dedicated to finding evidence of the Russian. Then he happened upon the smoldering village.

It pained him greatly that Zorro had been no less absent than the soldiers. After a cursory patrol of the Plaza the previous evening, Zorro had returned to his lair for study and training. In addition to the formidable weapons, the special crate of Japanese artifacts had contained documents and equipment relating to *karate,* one of a variety of ancient martial arts. This impressive style of hand-to-hand combat, he believed, would complement his skills as a swordsman.

Upon first glance, a practical fighter such as Zorro scoffed at the idea of stances, formal preparations intended to be made at the start of a battle. What enemy would pause in his attempt to shoot an opponent while he settled into a proper fighting stance? But as Diego came to understand the notions of focus and balance, the overall system of *karate* became clearer to him. Training in the martial arts would give Zorro greater speed and agility, and the unconventional style would give him yet another trump card to play against the tyrannical forces he battled in Los Angeles.

But this was for the future. Also, he admitted to himself, his training would mostly be considered imperfect by those responsible for the documents he studied. He would have no formal training. For one, Zorro lacked a *dojo*, a master from which to learn.

Diego mulled this all over as he rode back to his father's *hacienda* and continued to Zorro's hidden lair. As he tied up the Arabian near the entrance, Diego caught site of Tornado grazing in the small valley tucked beyond the Joshua trees. It was a rare and peaceful moment. Normally, the stallion's pounding hooves echoed the thundering of his spirit. Even in repose, however, Tornado emanated an undeniable power.

Diego looked down at the Arabian on which he rode. By any other standards, this was one of the finest horses his father—or anyone in the *pueblo* for that matter—owned. Still, compared to Tornado, the Arabian was a pack horse. The magnificence of Zorro's jet-black stallion was unparalleled. Watching Tornado now reminded Diego of the first time he laid eyes on the creature. . . .

It had been shortly after his return from school in Europe. Another piece to a puzzle he had not yet recognized was forming. He did know that many horses had been brought over early by Spanish settlers, and some had escaped into the wild. That day, riding out on the edge of his father's land, he had spied a herd running free.

Tornado stood out instantly among them: large eyes that gleamed with power, not the madness of many wild horses. His ebony form emerged from a billowing cloud of dust. The herd had spread out behind him, Tornado their majestic leader. The shimmering desert heat before the herd gave the impression that Tornado was emerging from some arcane, magical dimension.

Diego was instantly struck by a sense of destiny that he had felt few times since.

Joining with the thundering herd, Diego's own mare managed, barely, to pace Tornado. Diego knew this would not last and leapt upon the colt's back.

The colt reacted instantly and violently to the creature on his back, immediately bucking and leaping. The flexing sinews were the most powerful Diego had

ever experienced before—and since. Dust and sand
flew up in a funnel, inspiring Tornado's name. The
billowing cloud rose as the horse spun and leapt, trying to shake its rider. An onlooker would have seen
nothing less than cyclone rising from the desert.

Diego was lucky enough to hold on to the flowing
ebony mane as the rest of the herd passed. With one
mighty snap of his back, Tornado threw Diego. He
struck the desert floor hard. Dust and blood mingled
in his mouth. Spiny plants tore through his clothing.

Still, Diego was back on his feet in an instant. He
didn't want to let this amazing creature escape.

Miraculously, Tornado had gone nowhere. He
stood, the column of dust starting to settle. The colt
whinnied. Man and horse stared at each other, as if
preparing for a duel.

But the duel had already ended. Looking into the
colt's sharply intelligent eyes, he knew there would be
no more struggles. That had been a test. As Diego
approached, he was certain that he had passed that
test.

Tornado whinnied again and sighed as Diego
reached for his neck once more. As he attempted to
mount this time, the colt was skittish, but made no
attempt to throw him. The horse seemed to be telling
him, "You haven't broken me, we have chosen each
other."

And that's what Diego believed. That he and Tornado had chosen one another.

From that moment on, the horse had remained a
loyal friend, more so than just about any human being
save Bernardo. And their bond had an empathetic
quality that bordered on telepathic. Each was sensitive
to the other's moods. Tornado's reliability and his

trust in Diego, even during the most dangerous situations in which Zorro found himself embroiled, were absolute. Often, the stallion needed no direction, knowing what to do and where to go—and most importantly, how fast—with barely a word or gesture given.

Since their fateful meeting, he had been Tornado's only rider. Not even Bernardo had attempted to ride the stallion, although Diego assumed that in an emergency, this would be permitted—the horse and servant were old friends by now and obviously regarded each other with mutual respect. Any others, Diego expected, would suffer the same fate as he had that first day—that is, if they were even able to climb onto Tornado's back, which Diego thought unlikely. Blood and dust would be the only reward to anyone attempting to mount Tornado.

A whinny indicated the stallion had finally realized Diego was watching him. Tornado immediately galloped up to the Arabian, snorting at it not unkindly. Powerful and majestic as he was, Tornado was not given to bullying weaker horses, as other stallions tended to do.

Diego descended from the Arabian and led both horses to a second entrance of the lair, adjoining the hidden valley. Here, at another expertly camouflaged spot, he depressed a plate similar to the one near the front entrance to the secret lair. Muffled gears turned and a stone slide aside, revealing the lair's back entrance. Just inside was a wide tunnel containing bales of hay and a trough. Bringing the horses into the cool shade of the hidden stable, Diego fed and watered them both. Once this had been accomplished, Diego took a low, narrow passage that lead to the main chamber. Soon Bernardo would arrive, and they would discuss the events at the *pueblo*. He was interested to see what his old friend would make of the Dragon Riders.

He also wondered what the Dragon Riders would make of Zorro when they finally met.

Chapter 6

Arcadia Flores sighed as she packed her cart with an unusual number of unsold blankets, *serapes* and hand-woven garments. Though the marketplace was full of people today, few were buying. The return of Zorro and the attack of the creatures known as the Dragon Riders were the subjects of frenzied conversation on every corner of the square. Merchants' songs of praise for the beauty and quality of their wares fell upon ears filled with talk of recent events. Even the roasting meats attracted more flies than hungry customers. Only the fortune tellers possessed desirable commodities: explanations of what these events portended, rituals of protection and visions of the future.

Arcadia tried to look upon the lack of customers as a blessing in disguise. Often, the prospect of selling one more blanket would tempt her to relax her rule

of returning home before sundown. That custom had
been born the night four costumed soldiers had cornered her in a deserted market stall after dark, seeking
to take more from her than just blankets or *pesos*.
Zorro had appeared, wraithlike, as if emerging from
a cloak of night itself, and drove away her attackers.
In the subsequent days, he had rescued Arcadia from
jail after that oaf Sergeant Garcia had unjustly incarcerated her. But these had merely served as a prelude
to the terrifying events looming in her future. The evil
Hidalgo el Cazador, the self-proclaimed Aztec healer
who was in truth a dangerously greedy slavemonger,
had already drugged and kidnapped her brother and
father, stealing their free will as easily and completely
as their material possessions. When his own diabolical
powers of persuasion failed to convince Arcadia of her
special place at his side, he relied on more conven-
tional means: he had her kidnapped, intending to
bend her to his will at all costs. Zorro had miraculously appeared again to rescue her from yet another
man who saw her only as a lump of clay to be molded
by his hands for his own evil pleasure.

Since the end of that ordeal, she had disciplined
herself to return home well before dark. Although Arcadia could take care of herself, she saw no point to
placing herself in unnecessary jeopardy, especially
while the mysterious Fox remained unaccounted for.
She never believed he had been dead—as the last one
to see him, she knew he had suffered no lasting injuries from his battle with Cazador. Physically, that is.
Also better than most, she knew that the Aztec's pen-
etrating gaze had been sharper and more dangerous
than the jeweled dagger he had wielded. Perhaps
Zorro, like Arcadia, had been mentally assailed in
ways that required more healing than a mere broken

limb would have. Whatever the case, she thought about him, prayed for him, and always felt his presence nearby, hovering like the guardian angel she thought him to be. The tale of his reappearance at the cantina had filled her with greater joy than she thought possible. Though she had not despaired for a moment, knowing for certain that he was alive and well brought golden sunshine to a life she did not realize had darkened.

Now, as Arcadia loaded the last stack of blankets onto her *carreta*, snatches of conversation drifted through the air over the general rumble of the crowd.

"They flew from the sky!"

"The fires were started by the flaming hooves of their stallions!"

"I hear they snatched a poor woman's child and carried it away."

With only one appearance, the Dragon Riders had already become a formidable presence in the *pueblo*. Soon, superstitious imaginations would make them towering creatures able to consume entire herds of horses, powerful enough to set the entire *pueblo* ablaze with the slightest breath. Foolish, Arcadia thought. Perhaps; but how foolish? She thought of the things she had seen. Just because a creature possessed the shape of a man did not mean it was not a monster. Hidalgo el Cazador had proven that.

It was then, out of the corner of her eye, that she saw the stranger. He hovered inconspicuously on the periphery of the market. By his apparent age, he could have been her father. A tattered uniform clung uncomfortably to his huge frame. Speaking to no one, he did not have the look of a buyer. Lurking in a shadow one moment, peering with false interest at a merchant's wares the next, he seemed to be trying to avoid the notice of the few soldiers among the crowd and succeeding for the most part. His presence was a beacon to which only she seemed to respond. Arcadia did not feel threatened by him, but his appearance was nevertheless unsettling.

She frowned. Yes, the decision to get an early start for home had been a good one.

Sitting on her wagon and prepared to drive her oxen up the road, she noticed a change in the mysterious stranger's expression. He had become alert, head cocked to the side as if trying to pick a single sound out of the din of the plaza.

In a moment, she was hearing it, too.

The sound wove its way in and around the voices of the marketplace like a ribbon. An ancient Yang Nah woman selling jewelry looked up from a customer and turned toward the new sound. Soon, the customer was entranced, the jewelry forgotten.

Then, as if under the spell of a lullaby, conversation in the marketplace died down, replaced by the haunting melody that drifted in from elsewhere. It sounded like a flute, but deeper. The people crowding the plaza were held in its thrall.

Then melody trailed off, leaving each listener to resolve the tune in his or her own mind. An expectant hush filled the plaza.

The spell broke as a fireball burst from the roof of a building overlooking the plaza. A monstrous shape materialized from the smoke and fire, as if born of the conflagration: the leader of the Dragon Riders. The crowd watched, stunned, as the dragon breathed a column of flame towards the square. Raising a claw, it pointed a talon in the direction of Arcadia Flores.

Arcadia thought she saw the smoke behind the Dragon Rider twitch. Then, a horse screamed in a stall near Arcadia, falling dead and crushing a table full of pottery.

The horse's owner, a middle-aged *mestizo* woman, screamed and the plaza exploded in panic, the lilting melody of before barely a memory.

Two of the Dragon Riders appeared on horseback and entered the marketplace at full gallop. The monsters had been frightening in the dead of night, but to those who had survived the attack on the village, the Dragon Riders were even more terrifying in the sunlight. Their skin was a deep crimson, the color of drying blood. The sunset reflected off their scales, giving each one a glowing corona, as if lava flowed in their veins.

Peasants scattered as the ebony horses plunged into the crowd. With a chilling roar, the vicious dragon used the torch he carried to begin setting stalls alight.

The laughing dragon, as before, dismounted from his horse, and began to wade through the crowd, swinging a long club before him, cackling. Those struck by the weapon fell to the ground like harvested wheat. The leader stood on the roof, surveying the plaza with arrogant majesty, framed in billowing smoke and flames. The feather-maned dragon was nowhere to be seen.

Arcadia had frozen where she sat. Around her, people ran and screamed, inadvertently trampling others who had been knocked to the ground in the midst of the chaos. The oxen reacted to the confusion with twitching tails. Arcadia feared the animals would bolt and injure someone in the process, so she spoke to them in a low, soothing voice as she tried to figure out a safe course of action. Of the few soldiers that had been stationed at the marketplace, most were stymied at the moment: they could not use their guns for fear of shooting someone in the crowd.

To her relief, other soldiers appeared not so paralyzed with indecision and banded together to confront the laughing dragon. Swords raised, they formed a seemingly impassable barrier. The Dragon Rider faced them, turning in a slow arc to size up his would-be attackers.

"Let's send it back to hell!" one lancer cried and the group closed in on its prey.

The laughing dragon at once adopted a defensive posture: slightly crouched, the wooden club held out across its body in both blood-hued claws.

The nearest soldier rushed forward.

Instantly, the club became a spinning blur in the Dragon Rider's grasp. With a crack, it connected with the side of the man's face, driving him to one side and into another soldier. The force sent them both to the ground in a tangle.

Arcadia, watching from her stall, could see that the remaining soldiers knew they were no match for the laughing dragon. But they were soldiers, after all, not cowards, and would not turn from the fight. Seeing that the monster might easily kill the men, Arcadia felt sorry for them.

The Dragon Rider's club continued to twirl like a deadly pinwheel, which he now turned on one of the brave soldiers. Driving one end into the gut of the swordsman, it knocked the blade from his hand as he doubled over, breathless. The laughing dragon followed with an upward blow to the face which knocked the soldier backwards into the crowd, where he landed unconscious.

With insane amusement, the laughing dragon once again took his stance and faced the final lancer, who had drawn his gun. At such close range, the man surely would hit his target, Arcadia thought. But the young soldier had clearly been unnerved by his opponent, and the gun trembled in the man's grasp. As his finger shakily tightened on the trigger, an unearthly cry from the Dragon Rider halted the lancer for one crucial moment. In that moment, the club knocked the gun barrel upwards, where the ball fired harmlessly into the air. The gun itself flew tumbling away.

Planting the club in the ground, the laughing dragon vaulted at the lancer, catching him squarely in the chest and sending him sailing through the air, he, too, disappeared into the roiling crowd.

Landing on his feet and bringing the club up once more, the demon could see that he had run out of opponents. Curiously, he stood erect, held the club to his chest and, facing the direction of his final adversary, gave a short, formal bow.

The solemn moment ended, and the demon turned to the heavens and screeched in triumph. Returning its attention to earth and the surrounding turmoil, the laughing dragon took a moment to chose its next path. Then the Dragon Rider strode forward, scattering the crowd before it with the deadly club.

Meanwhile, the vicious dragon had been making its way down Arcadia's side of the plaza, looting stalls and stuffing the stolen merchandise into a large burlap sack. Women would cower away at his approach, and any man foolhardy enough to challenge the Dragon Rider was quickly driven away by a flurry of blows.

Meanwhile, Arcadia was losing her battle to keep her oxen calm. Their jostling had nearly knocked her from the *carreta's* perch. If they could be kept from bolting for another few minutes, she might escape. The crowd was now thinning, but still gave the oxen no safe path to travel. Until then, her wagon was hemmed in. Her only other choice was to abandon the wagon and risk losing all her wares, either to the ensuing riot or to the Dragon Riders. This was no real choice for Arcadia. Best to stay where she was, she thought.

That decided, Arcadia understood that she did not need to stay out in the open. Without letting go of the reins, she crawled into the back of the wagon. Flattening herself as much as possible, she crawled among blankets and serapes, trying to hide herself under them. The wagon still rocked as fleeing peasants pushed past, and the oxen were far from calm, but she would be safe.

Unless, of course, the Dragon Riders decided to set fire to her wagon.

Arcadia shuddered but pushed away the thought. Where were the lancers? she wondered. The *cuartel* was not far away, surely they must know that the plaza was under attack. Then she remembered: earlier in the day, Sergeant Garcia had taken a large squad of soldiers into the desert in search of the Dragon Riders. Still others he had posted at the village where the Riders had initially attacked, in case they returned. Little could anyone have guessed that the marauders would strike within the *pueblo* itself. Arcadia could only hope Garcia's men would return from the desert before the marketplace was consumed by flames.

Suddenly, the *carreta* lurched to the side, more forcefully than before. Looking up, she saw the back of a man pressed against the side of the wagon. Then he shot forward, gone as if yanked quickly away by an invisible force. A harsh yell filled the air and the sound of a blow was heard, followed by a pained cry. The man sailed over the cart, over Arcadia, and to the side. A grunt signaled that he had hit the ground.

Then hands were upon her, scratching and pulling. Instinctively, she batted the hands away and sat up, finding herself abruptly face to face with the vicious dragon. Despite its expressionless face, the creature seemed surprised that instead of blankets, it had seized her instead. With a hideous cry, the vicious dragon began to drag Arcadia from the *carreta*.

Anger burned away any fear in an instant. Monster or no monster, she had suffered too much abuse at the hands of others to surrender to it any longer. Planting the soles of her sandals against the lower lip of the wagon, she resisted her attacker. Exerting pressure, she was able to pull backward, out of the dragon's grasp. It released her suddenly, sending her sprawling backwards onto the pile of blankets in which she had been hiding.

The vicious dragon was upon her in a moment. Another cry rose from beneath its impassive face and he leapt onto the wagon, deftly landing on the thin edge of the wagon's side with both feet.

Arcadia quickly clawed backwards against the blankets. They slid beneath her, slowing her progress. Not that there was far to go, or that she would have gotten very far in any event.

The dragon fell upon her, its claws digging at her clothing.

But Arcadia had claws of her own and brought her nails up into the creature. She would gut it if she could. Instead, her fingernails clicked harmlessly against its hard, crimson shell. The shock racked her fingers with pain.

The dragon continued to shred her blouse, growling hideously.

If she hadn't become certain that this Dragon Rider were human, Arcadia thought, its—now certainly, *his*—actions had convinced her utterly. She wondered how human, then, it really was—and brought her left knee up into the space between its legs.

This attack, too, was thwarted by the dragon's thick skin. Still, she elicited more of a reaction from her attacker this time. Swiftly, he adjusted his position, pinning her legs to the bottom of the *carreta*.

She was about to utter a foul curse when she saw what might save her. The dragon's joints. Of course, she thought. Even a beetle has soft joints. Otherwise, it would be a statue. And surely, this creature was no statue. And there, where the arm joined its shoulder, was a dark, unprotected spot. Where it could bend. Similar regions appeared at places corresponding to major joints of the limbs and body. The dragon could be injured.

Or so she hoped.

But first, she had to free her arms, which were similarly trapped.

Despite the arid conditions that day, Arcadia could still work up enough saliva to spit into the vicious dragon's face. Knowing it would not necessarily even feel her spit on its hard skin, she aimed for the holes from where the eyes peered out.

She spat, and for the first time, elicited exactly the response she desired. The rider raised one clawed hand to his face to wipe the spittle away, freeing Arcadia's right arm. Before he could trap her again, she jabbed her hand—with five long, painstakingly maintained red nails—unhesitatingly into the joint where the creature's leg joined the rest of its body. If she were wrong, she would have no more tricks up her now-shredded sleeve.

But she was right.

Her own sharp nails dug into what seemed to be very common flesh in the creature's inner thigh. It screamed and rolled to the side, away from her.

Arcadia rolled in the opposite direction, up and over the edge of the cart and fell to the ground. Immediately, she was kicked by passersby, but was able to quickly crawl under the cart.

As she had expected, by now much of the crowd that had been in the plaza had fled. The lead Dragon Rider still stood watch from above. The soldiers were nowhere to be seen.

There came a thump above her. The floor of the *carreta* bowed downward slightly. Above, the vicious dragon scanned the plaza, looking for her.

Standing in a cart could be dangerous, she realized. It could move suddenly, throwing one to the ground. With a smile, she removed two hairpins that had not been lost in the scuffle.

The bowed floor shifted above her. The vicious dragon was preparing to move on.

"I am sorry, my babies," Arcadia whispered. Then she jabbed a hairpin into the rump of each of her already agitated oxen. They bellowed and bolted forward suddenly. Arcadia had to roll out of the way to avoid the cart's wheels or being kicked by the oxen.

The *carreta* lurched out from under the vicious dragon, throwing him to the ground. Arcadia rose to run, but found that the Dragon Rider was lying still, limbs tangled, resembling a marionette hastily cast away by a child. What's more, its head had come off.

The sight was so startling that Arcadia instantly forgot the danger and turned to investigate.

A few feet away, the vicious dragon's head lay staring sightless from a burning stall. Its eyes were black, empty. The middle of the head was split from ear to ear, with the back piece angled away as if they had been joined at the top by hinges.

Arcadia frowned, for when she looked at the Dragon Rider's body, she found it still had a head, of sorts. A human head, as she had come to suspect was underneath the beetle shell. However, the rider's face was turned away and all she could see was a thick mat of straight black hair. Turning back to the stall, she found that the mask—for that's clearly what it had been—had caught fire. Whatever coated its surface was causing it to burn quickly. Arcadia's first thought was to rescue the mask, but the vicious dragon behind her moaned. She did not want to be near when the Dragon Rider awoke. Flight, then, seemed like the wise choice. Leaving the burning mask behind, she ran a few steps to her *carreta*, which had not traveled far. Oxen had short memory, even of pain.

Just then, the sound of many horses rose above the roar of the blazing marketplace. The soldiers had finally returned from the desert, though clearly, too late. The plaza was in ruins, stalls ransacked and the square strewn with the injured. The amount of damage these Dragon Riders had caused was unbelievable. Even so, how could three of them stand against an army?

But one was not standing, she realized. The vicious dragon had not yet regained consciousness. Perhaps there was one thing she could do before fleeing, she thought. Some of her blankets had been shredded in the fray and would bind the raider's hands and feet easily. This might give the soldiers at least one prisoner should the others escape.

Taking several ruined blankets, Arcadia began to tear out strips as she returned to the spot where the vicious dragon lay. Though he had not risen, the sound of his groaning told her that time was running short.

She stood over the dragon, ready to bind his hands. Suddenly, a roar from across the plaza stopped her. Arcadia spun toward the source of the noise: the lead Dragon Rider. Arcadia had forgotten about him. The leader had spotted her from his fiery perch. Smoke still creating an eerie curtain behind him, the Dragon Rider raised his claw and pointed at her. As before, the smoke twitched and before she could dive to safety, something sharp struck her in the shoulder. The shock and the pain sent her spinning to the ground, clutching the wound. Blood seeped between her fingers.

The rider atop the tiled roof pointed at her again and Arcadia hastily scrambled into a stall for shelter. Whether he had feigned attack or she had successfully avoided the strange bolt it seemed to be throwing, nothing struck her. However, the attack had given the vicious dragon time to recover, and he rose from the ground before her.

He looked at her, huddled and bleeding in the smoking stall. Arcadia was transfixed by his face: clearly that of a young man, with almond-shaped eyes and smooth, pale skin. His rage was unmistakable. Claws unconsciously opening and closing menacingly, he stalked toward her. Arcadia could do nothing to defend herself.

The lead Dragon Rider suddenly roared again, stopping the vicious dragon in his tracks. He looked to his leader, who spoke again, unintelligibly. The vicious dragon replied with agitation. Arcadia could recognize an argument, no matter the language. The leader only repeated his words more forcefully, and nodded in the direction of the approaching horses.

The young man glanced Arcadia's way once more and narrowed his eyes in fury. Clearly, he was being prevented from punishing her for besting him. Despite his anger, however, he favored her with a bow, as she had seen the laughing dragon earlier bow to his opponents. With a final scowl, the vicious dragon ran off across the plaza toward the building on which the leader stood.

The laughing dragon appeared from the opposite end of the plaza and followed Arcadia's attacker. The two disappeared around the back of the building.

With a thunder of hooves, twenty lancers on horseback entered the square, led by Garcia. Among the soldiers was the new one, the lancer who was related to Captain Monastario. Riding side by side, his tall, lanky form and that of the squat, rotund sergeant painted a picture that would be comical in any other circumstance.

From her hiding place in the smoldering market stall, Arcadia did not understand how the leader of the Dragon Riders could take lightly the threat of having over a dozen guns trained upon him, as he did now.

"You there!" Sergeant Garcia cried, pointing up at the Dragon Rider on the roof. "Come down from there this minute. You are under arrest. Resist and we will have no choice but to shoot."

"Why *aren't* we shooting?" snapped Gutierrez. "Can't you see what they've done?"

Garcia turned to the private in surprise at the outburst. "Your uncle is not here, soldier. I will not brook your insubordination. Even dragons must be given the chance to surrender before being shot at."

"You think these are dragons?" Gutierrez laughed. "And I am a *saguaro*." From across the courtyard, Arcadia thought the image appropriate. "No wonder The Fox has eluded you all this time. Some men think. Others act. You do neither."

"Even your uncle wouldn't approve of your conduct, Private." Garcia growled. The *commandante*'s support of the plan to capture Zorro had filled the young soldier so full of himself that Garcia thought he would burst. "He'll hear about this. Be assured—"

"Do something, you idiots!" Arcadia yelled from her hiding place. They seemed like an old married couple bickering over a tamale. The two men looked her way in surprise. "Stop arguing and do something! You're lucky they haven't escaped yet!"

"There's no cause for—" Garcia began, spinning his horse around to locate the source of the voice. But apparently, the Dragon Rider shared Arcadia's opinion of the men. He raised both hands and gestured toward the crowd of soldiers.

"*Que pasa?*" one soldier asked.

Suddenly, there came a thin whistling and two horses suddenly collapsed, dumping their riders to the ground. The other horses whinnied and reared back. The order of the soldiers was broken.

Arcadia looked back up at the Dragon Rider. Kneading the air with his claws in an elaborate gesture, fire and smoke rose around him as if summoned by incantation. He stepped backwards through it and was gone.

Even as they regained order, the soldiers were

amazed by what they had just seen. Gutierrez gaped at the spot where the Dragon Rider had stood only moments ago.

They almost didn't hear the sounds of galloping horses receding from the far side of the square.

Chapter 7

The Dragon Riders easily eluded the soldiers that pursued them from the marketplace. The arguing buffoons had provided them with enough time to lose themselves in the desert and the darkness. At first, it seemed they themselves were lost, but their meandering was only to throw off anyone who might be following them.

Hours later, certain they had not been pursued, the sinister quartet arrived at a newly-made trail, high in the mountains to which the low hills now gave way. The trail ran along a stream, which they followed to its source, a natural pool fed by a high waterfall. Here, the riders dismounted from their horses, tying them near the pool so their steeds could drink as they continued upward.

An arduous hike through low brush brought them above the waterfall and back along the stream that fed it. The mountain air was much cooler than that of the desert. And thinner. Soon, they approached a desolate spot that could likely have never been seen by human eyes. The trail dwindled to nothing at a great boulder covered with lichen.

The Dragon Riders stood before the boulder. Something dark sat hunched atop it. A low growl rumbled from the spot, eyes gleamed into darkness. It was some kind of large cat.

Ignoring the obvious danger, the lead rider swept aside the scrub to the left of the boulder and plunged ahead. As he did so, the others followed. The feathered dragon looked up at the boulder. The cat had melted away. Or perhaps it had slunk away to find a better perch from which to attack. At that thought, the Dragon Rider glimpsed the cat once more—a flash of spots and gleaming yellow teeth above them. Once they passed to the other side of the boulder, the cat disappeared entirely. Beyond the boulder, an impressive sight greeted them.

They stood before a hidden city.

It lay in a valley ringed by high mountaintops. The entrance past the boulder seemed the only path. Low huts populated the outer perimeter, and stone buildings—most in the early stages of construction—could be seen as one penetrated the settlement. Dominating the city, set back against a cliff face, was the ragged form of what would one day be a pyramid. Everywhere were ornate carvings of great cats—jaguars, like the ghostly sentry.

The Dragon Riders headed for the pyramid. On the way, they passed no one. This hidden city was dead, empty save for them and the master who brooded in the pyramid. Their employer.

Hidalgo el Cazador.

Inside the pyramid, the entranceway continued to the left. To the right, a sloping ramp lead down to a lower level. The Dragon Riders took the left passage, entering a large chamber. Sand entirely covered the floor below them, muffling their footsteps. Before them sat Cazador on his throne, which was carved from a great piece of granite, rising from the sand as if both had been stranded in the desert. The lack of symmetry in the jaguar carvings of the throne's legs and sides attested that it was as unfinished as the rest of the city.

Cazador appeared to be deep in contemplation, his chin resting on one fist. A spotted fur cloak swept back from a jaguar's-head clasp fastened about the Aztec's throat. A tunic of hammered metal adorned his compact but powerful upper chest, which was otherwise bare. But his physique was not the true measure of his power. The Aztec's bearing, regal and commanding even in repose, was but a spark compared to the inferno raging behind the priest's eyes.

When Cazador acknowledged the Dragon Riders, his gaze piercing their souls like the beam of a lighthouse, ghostly jaguars briefly appeared to flank the throne. A scar of a smile crossed the Aztec's face. Then the cats were gone again.

"Welcome," Cazador said grandly. "Another successful raid, I trust? Any sign of The Fox?"

Washi, the group's leader, removed his dragon mask and gave a bow. Miko and Baku followed suit; Tanuki, the vicious dragon, had lost his mask at the marketplace.

"No fox," Washi said simply.

Cazador turned his gaze to Tanuki and frowned. "You've been careless, Tanuki," he scolded in Japanese, shaking his head. "You give up the game too quickly."

"Restraint makes us careless!" responded Tanuki impudently, also in Japanese. He was the youngest of the group and trusted the master of this dead city the least—and feared him the most. "I am a soldier, and my sword was made for tasting blood and bone. We deserve greater honor than to be as common thieves."

The young man had stepped in front of Washi and faced Cazador directly. His eyes burned with menace. The older man put his hand on Tanuki's shoulder to restrain him, but Cazador appeared unruffled.

"Talk to your honorable leader, young one," Cazador told him, glancing at Washi. "The peasants are but lambs meant to be slaughtered, especially for my purposes."

Washi spoke up. "We will not kill these defenseless people. It would bring us grave dishonor."

"Whatever you do, make certain you are enough of a threat to flush out Zorro," Cazador commanded. The oldest samurai seemed slightly shamed by the implied rebuke, but did not reply. The Aztec now turned back to Tanuki, whose anger had not yet subsided. "In the future, you will show more self-control—both in the midst of battle and before me. Should you allow The Fox to elude me, I'll make certain the Dragon of your nightmares consumes you."

Tanuki pulled away from Washi's grasp and drew both of his swords. "Threaten me again, false priest," he challenged, "and I will cut you open so that your legs become tangled in your own entrails!"

"Tanuki!" Washi shouted, but a serene Cazador waved for him to keep back.

"A nasty image, young one," the priest said, without taking his eyes away from Tanuki. "A terrible way to die."

Soon, it was Tanuki would could not escape Cazador's gaze. The soldier tried to glare back, but then his eyes widened in fear. Before him, Cazador's head was changing. His eyes became large and black, with scaled lids. A great fin sprouted on his forehead as his nose became a great snout. Beneath, fangs sprouted, more real and hideous than those of Miko's mask. Smoke curled out of two nostrils and flames flickered from between pointed teeth.

Cazador had become the Dragon. A real dragon. Its clawed wings unfolding, it rose from throne. The Dragon opened its mouth, the furnace of its insides preparing to incinerate Tanuki as it had taken his family as a child. It had found him. Tanuki screamed and fell to the ground, preparing to die as others had before the fury of the Dragon.

The other samurai saw only Cazador sitting on his throne, the scar of his smile widening in cruel amusement.

His face in the sand, Tanuki was praying in Japanese.

Washi looked down at the terrified young man, then back at Cazador.

"Was that necessary?" He was the only one of the group who spoke Spanish. Having served a powerful and wealthy *shogun* in their native Japan, only he of the group possessed a formal education.

"For a soldier, Tanuki is remarkably insubordinate," Cazador replied, dismissing the groveling boy. He looked eagerly to Washi. "So tell me of your attack on the market tonight."

As Washi recounted the events earlier in the evening, Miko regarded Tanuki. The soldier's terror had subsided but he still seemed lost in his thoughts. Miko pitied him. Baku, as always, was oblivious. He had retired to the corner of the room and withdrawn his large, club-like weapon, a *shakuhachi*. Sitting, he brought the club to his lips and blew into one end. Working his hands over the openings along the *shakuhachi*'s length, a haunting melody came from it. The musician's smile became blissful and far away as he played. Miko thought his expression matched the meaning of his name, which was "dream-eater." He seemed to be dreaming constantly, even in the midst of a battle.

"And you, priestess, is there anything you wish to add?" Cazador was addressing Miko, whose attention had been drawn away by Baku's music.

"There is nothing more," she replied in Japanese. "The Fox, Zorro, who we call *Kitsune*, did not appear." She averted her eyes as she spoke. This was not out of reverence—she was a Shinto priestess in her own right, probably more legitimately than this man's claim to priesthood—but to avoid the power of his eyes.

His hand touched her chin, gently raising her head so that she could not avoid his probing gaze.

"It is no shame that you did not draw out El Zorro," Cazador told her, mistaking the reason she had bowed her head. "He will come eventually, I'm sure of it. He cares too much for the people you threaten."

Caught in his eyes, she felt his hand slide to her neck and stroke it. Then he released the tie that bound her hair into a ponytail. Her thick black hair, now free of the tie, spread down across her back like an ebony waterfall. The hand caressed her hair, her back . . .

Miko stepped backwards and looked down. Cazador lowered his hand—it had never left her chin. Her ponytail remained bound. The Aztec's scar smile had become slightly more wicked.

"El Zorro will come. Eventually." Cazador rose from his throne. "And when he does, you will subdue him as instructed and bring him to me."

Anger started to seep from the Aztec as he remembered the final conflict with Zorro that had robbed him of everything: his followers, his pyramid, his gold. How Zorro had entombed him alive. For these things, Zorro must die.

"At that time, I will punish him as he would have punished me. He will be sacrificed to the old gods." Cazador's gaze seemed to pierce the stone walls of the pyramid as he looked toward the dead city. "I will put him to death so that this place will have life. I will again descend upon Los Angeles, and its people will give themselves to me utterly. They will complete this"—he gestured to grandly to the sky—"a secret that even Zorro could not discover—a city I was building even as the main force of the workers was completing the great pyramid of Los Rayos del Sol."

The Aztec turned to the Dragon Riders.

"I will have my revenge, and you will make it possible. And you will be rewarded—with riches as well as power over all those miserable souls in Los Angeles."

He walked over to Tanuki, who had finally stood, quietly taking in Cazador's speech. Baku had even stopped playing music to pay uncharacteristic attention.

Grasping the boy by the shoulders, Cazador told him, "Your sword *will* taste the blood you seek."

* * *

The smell of sulfur was strong.

Zorro examined the roof of the adobe where the Dragon Rider had stood. A wide arc scorched the tile. Nearby, caught in a crevice, was the charred stub of a torch. Evidently, chemicals much like those he used for his own fireworks had been spread on this section of roof and ignited. The resulting flash probably accounted for the sudden, fiery appearance of the Dragon Rider. An accomplice would have been needed, however, to ignite the fire and continue feeding it with the proper chemicals to maintain the fiery effect.

A second Dragon Rider on the roof also accounted for the first rider's "power" to shoot bolts from his hands. They were, of course, not bolts at all, but arrows, as an examination of the felled horses had revealed. Hidden low and behind the smoke screen, an archer needed only to fire on cue from the dragon's gesture.

He thought of Arcadia Flores, who had also been struck by an arrow. Don Diego would contrive to speak to her tomorrow. With her farm so near to the de la Vega *hacienda*, their friendship had flourished since Zorro had "brought" her to the house. He knew that Arcadia had not been seriously injured—the arrow had only grazed her shoulder.

Like a spider, Zorro descended the uneven face of the adobe silently. Horse droppings and many hoofprints were found on the ground below. At least two horses had been waiting.

For supernatural creatures, Zorro thought that they seemed particularly in need of earthly transportation and ordinary weapons. But this brought him no nearer to discovering the Dragon Riders' motives or identities. He lacked any evidence other than the burned roof and the fanciful descriptions of superstitious eyewitnesses. One thing was certain, they were masterful in their ability to confound pursuit. Their trail had gone cold by the time Zorro, an experienced tracker, had attempted to hunt down the Dragon Riders.

The bandits' foray into the city, within minutes of the *cuartel,* had been bold. Once again, four of them—the three seen by the crowd at the market plus the dragon leader's accomplice—had caused a great deal of destruction.

Zorro felt ashamed. Again, he had failed to protect the peasants of Los Angeles. Had he not been investigating the village that the Dragon Riders had attacked the previous night, far from the center of town, he might have actually happened upon them here.

Meanwhile, Zorro had another distraction. The Russian from the earlier evening, whom Zorro had been unable to locate, had been arrested by Garcia. The stranger had been spotted at the marketplace just prior to the attack. Having failed to apprehend the Dragon Riders, Garcia's men had chanced upon the Russian and accused him of being the fourth Dragon Rider. Though Zorro sensed this was unlikely, he supposed it was not impossible.

The timing of the Russian's appearance and that of the Dragon Riders seemed almost too close to be a coincidence. However, this in itself was not proof of guilt. For now, though, Sergeant Garcia seemed justified in detaining the Russian while a fair investigation was conducted. Remembering his pledge at the cantina, Zorro decided to keep an eye on the Russian, prepared to speed justice along.

With his sword, if necessary.

Chapter 8

The next day, *Commandante* Monastario tried for several minutes to speak to the only prisoner that inhabited either of the jail's two cells: Gutierrez's Russian. After many different tacks, each failing to elicit a coherent response, Monastario had even attempted to adopt a paternal tone when addressing the prisoner. To Sergeant Garcia and Private Gutierrez, their *commandante* had resembled some lewd codger trying to lure an innocent *señorita* into a dark alley more than anyone's kindly old father. Whichever interpretation was more accurate, the prisoner responded with his customary blank stare. No one was sure whether he could not understand or simply chose not to respond.

Finally confounded, *Commandante* Monastario turned away from the jail cell with an annoyed "hmph." The prisoner understood that well enough and lay back on his bed, its metal frame groaning in protest for having to support a man much too large and heavy for it. The Russian's expression remained unchanged, regarding the ceiling with as much mute attention as he had the *Commandante*.

"I've had better conversations with statues!!" Monastario huffed, leading Garcia and Gutierrez to the opposite end of the room. The trio stopped at the desk where the head of the prison detail, today Gutierrez, usually sat. "Well?" he asked, tapping his foot.

"Sometimes he does speak, *Commandante*," Garcia finally said, feeling compelled to speak.

"What does he say?"

"*No sé*," Garcia admitted. "We don't understand the language."

"Imbecile!" Monastario snapped immediately. "Then he might as well not be speaking. If you think the seat of your trousers has worn thin, try my patience. Which you do. Constantly!"

The *commandante* turned to his nephew, who stood waiting to be recognized.

"What do you have to say, then, Gutierrez?"

"We must put the Russian on trial immediately sir. As a traitor, spy, and murderer!"

Monastario rolled his eyes. He knew the litany by now. "And then Zorro will be ours, yes? He will emerge to save the Russian and, with the carefully laid trap, be at our mercy."

"Exactly!" Gutierrez cried, triumphant. It had all gone even more splendidly than planned.

"I think you are learning too much from Sergeant Garcia, here," Monastario told him. The next words hit Gutierrez like blows to the stomach. "The plan has failed."

The younger soldier was indignant. "But . . . but . . . we have the Russian!"

Monastario adopted the tone of an adult talking to a very small, and not very bright, child. This portrayal was much more successful than the fatherly character of before.

"The plan was to capture the Russian in order to draw out Zorro. But if the Russian is indeed linked to the raiders, as he may well be, Zorro will not try to save him, because he is harming those The Fox has sworn to protect. Zorro is no rash fool." Then with a smirk, Monastario added, "Like you appear to be, nephew."

Garcia suppressed a smile. It was gratifying to see Gutierrez put into his place. After all, it was the private's insolence at the scene that had allowed the remaining Dragon Riders to escape the plaza. Challenging his superior officer during the apprehension of dangerous villains. It had been an outrage, a disgrace! Perhaps it would have been better to ignore the private instead of responding, Garcia thought briefly. The *commandante* blamed them both for the argument that allowed the Dragon Riders to escape. Maybe so, Garcia thought—but the private had started it!

"Find someone who can speak Russian, Garcia," Monastario ordered. "This man must be able to tell us something."

"Yes, sir."

"And you," Monastario said turning to Gutierrez. "You look like a child who's had his candy taken away. Stop pouting and think of something else. If you are defeated by my words that easily, how would you prevail against Zorro?"

"If he were before me, we would not speak!" Gu-

tierrez spat. "My sword piercing his lungs would prevent that!"

"Of course," Monastario replied drolly. "Meanwhile, find another route to your dramatic scenario.
The Russian is useless as bait."

With that the *commandante* turned and left the jail,
acknowledging the pair no further. Both watched him
go gladly, for their own reasons.

"Only one person in Los Angeles is worldly and
educated enough to speak to this man," Garcia said
finally, mostly to himself.

"Who?" Gutierrez asked sullenly, not really interested. He had his own problems.

"Don Diego de la Vega," Garcia replied. "His father sent him to Europe for study. And for once, his
studiousness may actually be useful to someone. Certainly it is of no use to his father."

"Don Diego," Gutierrez spat, removed for a moment from his foul mood. He remembered seeing the
bookworm at the burned-out village the previous day.

"I will ask Don Diego to assist us in our investigation," Garcia informed the private. "Though of
course, I have no authority to order his compliance."

"No authority," Gutierrez repeated in a low voice.
His foul mood had returned, thinking of the privilege
enjoyed by a soft-shelled crab like Don Diego while
he, a true man, kept company with imbeciles like Garcia and suffered constant humiliation from his own
uncle. And here the military was expected to go groveling to this *caballero* for assistance. He should be *ordered* to help. Any man would believe it his solemn
duty to obey such a summons. Yet Don Diego would
be treated like a ruffle-shirted dignitary, simply because he could read more words on a bottle of vodka
than the next man. He bet Diego could not even

stomach a drop of the contents of such a bottle.

"Private!" Garcia shouted, bringing him to attention. "I said stay and watch the prisoner," Garcia ordered. "Did you hear me this time?"

"*Sí*," Gutierrez replied with a weak salute. This was enough for Garcia, who left to summon Don Diego. The private took a long look at the Russian, who stared back evenly. Gutierrez finally scowled at the man and turned away. He could not bear to look upon a prisoner who seemed less miserable than he himself felt at this moment.

"It seems that besides these so-called Dragon Riders, I'm the most wanted man in the *pueblo*," Don Diego told Arcadia Flores as he entered the salon. He had just agreed to Garcia's request, made through a lancer who had just departed the *hacienda,* to attempt communication with the Russian.

In a gesture indicative of their growing friendship, Diego had brought Arcadia to the *hacienda* to make certain she was recovering from her wound. She gladly responded to his invitation, always happy to visit such a large and luxurious house. Don Diego's concern was touching, she thought. He asked many questions about her experience, seeming particularly fascinated by the mask.

"I wish I had rescued it from the fire." Arcadia had told him. "I would have displayed it on a post in front of my house. The Dragon Riders would think twice about attacking someone who had beheaded one of their kind."

The woman entranced Diego. She could look back upon her experience with humor. He admired that quality.

"Still, I'm certain I would have been much too

frightened to even think about saving the mask. I prefer to read of adventures, not actually live them." Diego gave a theatrical shudder. "But tell me more about the mask and its rider."

He coaxed her into a detailed description of the mask, from the shape of the mouth to the workings of the clasp. Arcadia seemed to appreciate an audience.

"Have you spoken to Sergeant Garcia of what you've seen?" Diego asked. "I am sure the military could use all available information on the Dragon Riders."

Arcadia wrinkled her nose in distaste. "Sergeant Garcia has avoided me since our dispute. I don't know if he's embarrassed by me or afraid of me." ·

"Probably both!" Diego laughed. Arcadia's defiance of Garcia had once placed her in a jail cell, from which Zorro had freed her—much to the sergeant's embarrassment. "Now if you will forgive me, I must prepare to go to the *cuartel*. I am so glad you are not seriously injured."

"You are very kind," Arcadia answered. "Much more than I deserve."

Diego laughed. "Nonsense. There are no boundaries to the kindness one can show to a friend."

With that, Arcadia Flores left, escorted by one of Diego's ranch hands. He was staring after her when · he realized he himself was being watched. Turning, he found Bernardo regarding him with a mix of amusement and concern. He looked through the window at Arcadia, now a speck in the distance, then back at Diego.

"Yes," sighed Diego, "I am rather fond of her. But under the circumstances, it is not meant to be." He shrugged. Bernardo held up a piece of paper and Diego's cloud lifted immediately. "What have we here?"

A series of snarling faces raged at Diego from the page. Closer examination revealed drawings of a single dragon mask, each sketch showing it from a different angle. While Arcadia Flores told her story to Diego, describing the mask in detail, Bernado had sat in an adjoining room bringing her descriptions to life.

"It's no doubt these bandits struck fear in even the soldiers," Diego remarked. "The countenance is frightening even though it is only a drawing."

Bernardo signed elaborately.

"So it's not even a mask, but a helmet, worn by whom?" Bernardo repeated a gesture with which Diego was only barely familiar. "Samurai. Of course. It looks like we are not the only purveyors of Japanese form and function. They certainly protected the Dragon Riders, as well as frightening the peasants. And from what Arcadia Flores says, I believe that her attacker, as well as the others, came from Japan as well."

A look of concern on Bernardo's face spoke more eloquently than his signing.

The expression was reflected in Diego's face. "Good question. Traveling across an ocean seems unlikely if the goal is simply to steal some blankets, or even to terrorize simple people. Which brings us to the Russian."

Bernardo agreed he was an enigma.

"Arcadia saw him at the marketplace just prior to the attack. He is linked, I feel, but not in any way I can figure just yet. Luckily, as Sergeant Garcia surmised, I picked up some Russian during my studies abroad. I should be able to gain some information from him."

Diego looked at the drawings again. Though the

sketches had been rendered in quick strokes, they were still quite detailed.

"Your skills amaze me, old friend," Diego remarked as he prepared to travel to the *cuartel*. "While you consider the reasons samurai would be in Los Angeles, I will try to solve the riddle of our Russian visitor."

Chapter 9

"Don Diego de la Vega, *gracias*. Your assistance in this matter is greatly appreciated." Garcia was effusive in his thanks. Gutierrez simply stood by, not smiling.

"I don't know what I can do," Diego shrugged. "I learned very little Russian in Europe."

"Any amount would be more than what we poor soldiers know," Garcia told him. Diego thought he saw the private make an unpleasant face. "And although we believe that this man is connected with the Dragon Riders, it would be unjust to assume his guilt without at least an attempt to let him explain himself, don't you think?"

"Your desire for fairness is admirable," Diego answered. "It is why I'm here, although as you know, I am usually loath to get involved in affairs. I must say it is a bit unsettling to find myself within the walls of a jail, and so near a criminal."

"Let us find out if he is indeed a criminal," Garcia

responded. He extended his hand toward the cell housing the Russian. "This way. Let me bring you a stool."

The Russian watched them enter from where he sat at the edge of his narrow bed, the only furnishing within the cell. The packed dirt floor and white walls were featureless. Appropriate, Diego thought, for a man whose expression was as unreadable as the cell was bare.

Diego was led to the middle of three stools and sat facing the Russian. He was about to speak when a light, unnoticed by the lancers, crept into the prisoner's eyes. The same special awareness that Zorro had sensed the night of the Russian's arrival had returned. Then the light winked out—no, not winked out, but was hooded. Diego could see it shining at the edges of his guarded expression.

Gutierrez and Garcia had taken the stools flanking Diego, who suddenly felt very crowded.

"Please ask him his name, Señor de la Vega," asked Garcia.

Appearing to dredge up rudimentary Russian—a language in which he was actually quite fluent—Diego haltingly asked the Russian his name.

The man in his cell said nothing, appearing not to understand. Then he looked pointedly at Garcia and Gutierrez, frowned, and looked back at Diego.

Gutierrez rose. "We can force him to speak to you!"

The Russian's eyes never left Diego.

"Now, now," Diego interjected. "I believe he is simply nervous to speak in front of you. If you would be so kind to excuse us, I might have better luck alone."

"Surely that wouldn't be wise, Señor de la Vega," Garcia told him. "What if he were to attack you?"

Diego laughed. "I trust your bars are strong enough. I'll sit back against the wall."

"Señor de la Vega is right," Gutierrez said. "We

wouldn't understand what he was saying anyway, since we're poor, uneducated soldiers." Don Diego pretended not to notice the implied insult.

"Are you sure you will be all right on your own?" Garcia seemed truly concerned for Diego, although there was a great worry for his own hide as well. If any harm befell the son of the area's wealthiest landowner on Garcia's watch, the disaster would be tenfold for the poor sergeant.

"Surely you won't be far," Diego laughed, trying to put Garcia at ease.

"We'll be right here." Garcia told him as he and Gutierrez repaired to the prison watch table.

The two soldiers sat facing the cell, Garcia smiling amiably, Gutierrez with an anxious expression, waiting for the interview to begin. When Diego turned back to the cell, he could feel the eyes of the lancers like a swarm of mosquitoes on the back of his neck. The Russian remained silent. After nearly a minute, the awkwardness nearly stifling, Diego turned quickly back to Garcia.

"Perhaps I could suggest—" he began, but the sergeant, whose smile had choked on the oppressive silence, was ahead of him for once.

"Of course, we'll be right outside." Garcia and Gutierrez rose and exited the jailhouse, the sergeant barely squeezing between the door's wood frame and the private ducking to prevent striking his head.

The two lancers finally gone, Diego could finally talk to the prisoner. Before he could speak, however, the Russian stood and bowed deeply, sweeping his hand in front of him.

"Yuri," he said, rolling his 'r' in a deep, rumbling bass voice.

Impressed with the man's graciousness, Diego stood and bowed similarly and introduced himself.

"Are you indeed from Russia?" Diego asked in Russian, pretending to have to search for the right words.

The prisoner shrugged, but said nothing.

Diego stared at the expressionless man, learning nothing. "Where are you from, then? Why have you come here?"

Yuri sat back down on the edge of the bed. Was the interview over so quickly? Diego thought. The prisoner glanced at the door once more.

"The two fools listen at the door, of course," he finally growled in Russian, turning back to Diego. "But they understand nothing, so speak fluently in my tongue, as I know you can."

"How do you know this, sir?" Diego made no more attempt to hide his proficiency at Russian. The soldiers on the other side of the door gave no sign they could distinguish Diego's formerly halting speech with his current flawless delivery. Exactly as the prisoner had sensed.

"Secrets can only be kept from those with no interest in the truth," Yuri replied enigmatically.

Rather than revealing himself, Yuri drew his cloak of mystery around him more tightly. Diego shifted in his seat as he tried to figure what to say next. Yuri waited patiently.

"Tell me about yourself, Yuri," he said to the other man. "Or about the bandits, if you know about them. Are you one of these Dragon Riders? They believe you are. That is why you have been detained."

"The *ronin*." The deep, rolling 'r' made the word beautiful, although Diego was unfamiliar with the term. Instead of asking for an explanation, however, he now waited, like Yuri had done before, until the other continued speaking.

The prisoner rose and walked slowly toward the bars. "*Ronin* are the wave men, the masterless samurai."

His hands gripped the bars as firmly as he held Diego in his steady gaze. "The feudal society of Japan is disintegrating, leaving many skilled samurai without lords to serve, making them *ronin,* wandering the countryside."

"Is there not enough countryside in Japan for these *ronin* to wander?" Diego asked ironically. "Why have they come here?"

"I do not know." Yuri answered in a rare moment of uncertainty.

"And why are you here?" Diego asked. "How do you know these things?"

"I am Cossack," he proclaimed. "It is reason enough to be anywhere."

Diego had heard of Cossacks, tribes of fierce warriors from the eastern steppes of Europe. They served in the Czar's army and a great, natural ferocity was attributed to them as a people. Wandering and nomadic by nature, this one Cossack had wandered far indeed.

"I have traveled Japan," Yuri continued. "I've seen *ronin.*"

"But you are otherwise unconnected with these particular *ronin.*"

"*Da.*"

"Then I will proclaim your innocence immediately," Diego told him, rising excitedly. He wished to continue his conversation with Yuri, but not here, not within the confines of this dreary jail. Not all rescues needed to be dramatic affairs, he thought, with Zorro flinging grenades and lashing out with his whip. Sometimes, a simple word would suffice. A person as ordinary as Diego could sometimes ensure justice.

"Wait," Yuri said reaching out, his great forearm barely squeezing between the bars.

"What's wrong?" Surprised, and fearless because of

his conviction of the prisoner's innocence, he stepped forward. Within reach of the Cossack, the meaty hand seized Diego's shoulder. The second shot out from between the bars and took hold of the other.

"What—?" Diego could barely speak as Yuri pulled him toward the bars and began to shake him violently.

"No!" the Cossack cried loudly in Russian. "You cannot, must not, save Yuri."

"What are you doing?" Diego asked, attempting in vain to pull himself out of the Cossack's grasp.

"Call for help. Yuri attacks you!" The statement was too curious for Diego to be afraid. The man was shaking him like a rag doll and all he felt was confusion.

"Save Yuri and the masked man is doomed!" Yuri was pleading, desperate. Still, Diego was too mystified to cry out for help. "Believe in my guilt, if not of being Dragon Rider, then of other crimes. And if you won't believe, then make the buffoons believe! The tall one, he feels threats too deeply to forget."

As if on cue, Gutierrez and Garcia burst into the room.

"Unhand him immediately!" Sergeant Garcia cried.

With a baton, Gutierrez struck Yuri across his right arm. The prisoner withdrew in silent pain. Diego flew backwards unexpectedly, stumbling over the remaining stool, upsetting it.

"Are you hurt, Señor de la Vega?" Garcia cried in horror. He immediately began dusting off Diego with the flat of his sweaty palm. Diego stepped backward to escape having grease smeared on his shirt.

"I am fine, sir, simply surprised." This was no lie. Diego was nearly in shock. But not in pain. The scene must have looked more violent than it had been. Yuri had not injured him in the least.

"We should have warned you of the man's erratic

behavior. He has been unpredictable since our first encounter with him in the cantina some nights ago." The sergeant seemed quite upset. "I was remiss in my duties to allow that to have happened. *Dios mio!*"

Diego saw what he was getting at. "Fear not, I'll not report the incident. Think of how my father would react if he heard about this misadventure! No need for either of us to suffer, if you catch my meaning, Señor."

Sergeant Garcia was visibly relieved.

"What did the man say, Senor?" asked Gutierrez suddenly. He more than Garcia seemed anxious for information from the prisoner. "It looked like a desperate plea for help. He is innocent after all, is he?"

Diego looked into the cell. Yuri had retreated to his bed and sat there stolidly once more. Then he looked back up at Gutierrez, who stood like a puppy waiting for a table scrap.

"He is no innocent," Diego astonished himself by saying. Gutierrez reacted more visibly, his jaw nearly dropped to the floor. "He spent much of our little talk bragging about his exploits with the so-called Dragon Riders. And that after they come to rescue him, how he would hunt me down."

Gutierrez was speechless for several seconds. "So he really *is* one of them?"

"We finally caught a real criminal!" Garcia marveled. The others ignored him.

"By his own admission," Diego told them. "Now if you don't mind, I'd like to return to my *hacienda*. I would prefer not to be here if the Dragon Riders did suddenly appear."

The comment immediately quelled any pleasure Garcia had found in having captured a criminal. He looked out the window fearfully, as if expecting to see three dark horsemen riding in their direction. The plaza appeared peaceful enough, however.

For his part, Gutierrez looked as if Diego's guilty verdict had condemned him and not the prisoner.

Diego smoothed his clothes. "I commend you on catching one of these bandits. For the sake of us all, I hope you catch the rest before long."

"Allow me to escort you home so that you may report any pertinent details that would assist our effort," Garcia offered.

"Of course."

"Gutierrez," Garcia ordered. "Get a detail of men to come with us, so that our journey will be a safe one."

"Yes, sir, Sergeant." Almost in a daze, Gutierrez went to carry out Garcia's orders.

As he and the sergeant waited to return to the de la Vega hacienda, Diego reflected on the final moments of his encounter with mysterious prisoner. Yuri had acted and spoken strangely, but it was Gutierrez who had unwittingly provided the explanation.

The lancer evidently had hoped that Diego would proclaim the man innocent. This could have saved the Yuri's life, bringing the death of another: Zorro. The prisoner's final words had been the clue. If the Cossack had remained incarcerated after a declaration of innocence, Zorro would have been expected to rescue him. His own words at the cantina—the "threat" that Gutierrez had remembered—meant to protect the stranger had backfired. He had not been jailed in connection to the Dragon Riders, but specifically to draw Zorro into a trap.

Yuri knew that once branded guilty by Diego, an important and respected local figure, Gutierrez's plans would be foiled. The soldiers would be no closer to capturing either Zorro or the Dragon Riders.

But this was not all good news, for it left difficulties for Diego as well. The Russian was still in jail and still innocent of crimes associated with the Dragon Riders. But any attempt by Zorro to free an apparently guilty man would tarnish his reputation for fighting injustice.

Regardless of the man's penchant for self-sacrifice, however, Diego would not allow the stranger to come to harm, Zorro *could not* allow it.

Pretending to have been shaken by his experience at the jail, Diego barely spoke to the soldiers that escorted him home. In truth, his mind was racing to solve the problems the Russian had created. He knew that in the current climate of fear created by the Dragon Riders, Monastario would act quickly to show the citizens of the pueblo he had matters under control. Even if this was patently false. The commandante would act quickly to sentence the stranger to death. Then there was the Dragon Riders themselves to worry about.

At that thought, the spark of an idea ignited in Diego's brain. Perhaps someone would ride to Yuri's rescue after all.

Not Zorro, of course, but someone . . .

Chapter 10

The thinking, the planning, was driving him crazy. Action was now demanded.

Not long ago, hours after returning from the *cuartel*, Bernardo had come to him in a panic. Diego's false pronouncement of guilt had condemned Yuri. He was to be executed at sunset that same day, even sooner than Deigo had expected. He bitterly thanked his position in society for the even greater speed with which Monastario acted to punish the prisoner. Sometimes influence was more dangerous to wield than a sword.

The Cossack had implored Diego to condemn him in a gesture designed to save Zorro from Gutierrez's trap. But as the day wore on, Diego realized that Yuri had no alternate plan to save himself. He knew he would die. A stranger, alone in a foreign land, accused of violent crimes, he would die mourned by no one.

Whether to atone for past crimes, actual or imagined, or as a martyr to a cause unfathomable to Diego, Yuri had resigned himself to fate.

But where fate included Zorro, men did not die needlessly. Zorro would not mourn Yuri's death—he would prevent it.

As he rode toward the square, the wind causing his cape to billow, Tornado's muscles churning beneath him, he did not plan so much as prepare for action.

The question had been one of how to rescue Yuri without tainting the mission and reputation of Zorro? The answer had finally come.

Zorro smiled to himself. Was not the fox the very spirit of wiliness?

The Dragon Riders rode silently toward Los Angeles. Miko observed the grim expression set in Tanuki's face. He was only nineteen years old. Though he was fiery and undisciplined, Miko pitied him.

At the hidden city, Cazador had lashed out at the boy once more. Tanuki again crumbled to the ground, crying out the names of his family. They had perished in a fire when he was very young, old enough only to understand they were dead. The dangerous enchantment of Cazador's eyes could bring this memory from the depths of Tanuki's mind and make him relive it again, but with more terror each time it surfaced.

She wondered why Washi, their leader, did not kill Cazador. He obviously felt like a father to the boy, and Tanuki heeded him like no other. But then she herself would look into the Aztec's eyes, feel his gaze boring into her, and understand. With his mind, Cazador could keep them all at arm's length. Or further, if he wished, yet still maintain his hold over them.

Meanwhile, they rode toward the city to flush out The Fox. Their goal seemed so clear in Cazador's presence, yet away from him it made so little sense—and seemed so very dangerous.

In Japan, *kitsune* were much more than animals to chase for sport, they were the messengers of Inari, the *kami* of certain crops. As a Shinto priestess in Japan, one of few roles that would allow a woman to learn the arts of war and men, she had supervised ceremonies concerning the placement of *kitsune* statues. They were powerful spirits who would reward fealty and punish faithlessness.

And sometimes, their punishment would be spiritual possession.

Was this Zorro simply a man who took the fox's name? Or was this a fox spirit residing in the body of a man?

Regardless, challenging The Fox did not bode well.

A festival atmosphere pervaded the courtyard outside the *cuartel*. Crowds of people milled before what appeared to be a grandstand from which dignitaries would make flowery speeches. However, instead of a podium, this grandstand featured a gallows. And unlike a podium with a long-winded bureaucrat, this would command rapt attention.

A loyal audience had consistently turned out for the numerous public floggings over the years. Even more would gather to witness the occasional hanging of a bandit, or, more commonly, an Indian who had run afoul with the law. But interest in these had waned of late; Indians on the wrong side of colonial law were common. Usually they were just desperate natives out to avenge the deaths of loved ones at the hands of their Spanish oppressors, so the novelty had worn off.

However, the execution of a foreigner such as this so-called Russian was a unique experience. A true criminal—one of the Dragon Riders—and a creature who spoke, dressed and acted differently from them. He was a rare butterfly captured and placed in a killing jar.

As an undercurrent to the excitement, many were disappointed in the foreigner's guilt. Like Gutierrez, they would have expected an appearance by Zorro had the condemned man been treated unfairly. Unlike Gutierrez, however, those in the crowd wishing for Zorro to appear wanted only to witness the spectacle of the masked swordsman in action. Tonight, though, they resigned themselves to thinking there would be no Zorro. The well-known Don Diego de la Vega had pronounced the man guilty. His own fairness was well known, and he would not make such an accusation lightly. No doubt his word would have reached ears of the mysterious Zorro, as it had spread to the large crowd in the courtyard. Zorro would not rescue a man guilty of the crimes they had endured in the last few days.

So, despite the fact that Zorro would not appear, at least they would witness the hanging of a criminal. The crowd buzzed in anticipation.

Zorro dismounted from Tornado and led him by the reins through the maze of backstreets of the *pueblo*. They were, of course, no maze to him—he had memorized every turn and dead end. He would easily elude pursuers, should it come to that this evening.

He didn't think it would.

The streets were deserted, with the bulk of the population in the courtyard to watch the execution. For once, the morbid fascinations of others served his purpose. An adobe now rose above him and Zorro let go of the reins. No need to tie Tornado up; the stallion would not stray. Besides, the horse needed to be unfettered so he could to ride to the rescue when called—or escape on his own in a worst-case scenario.

Grasping its woven leather grip, Zorro detached his whip from the loop on his belt. Then, with a gentle flick of the wrist, cast it upward, where the tip wrapped itself around a *viga*, the peeled log beam jutting from the roof of the adobe. A quick tug and the loop caught itself firmly, tightening around the timber. Zorro gave the whip a steady pull downward. It would hold him. With that, he quickly ascended, hand-over-hand up the length of the whip, his feet finding traction against the rough adobe walls. Soon, he grasped the *viga* itself, swung himself feet first onto the roof, and landed solidly. Almost unconsciously, he untwisted the whip and pulled it up behind him. It was neatly looped and attached to his belt within seconds.

Hunkering down on the sloped roof, he started to climb, the scabbard of his sword clicking quietly against the fired clay tiles. Crawling slowly to prevent any loose tiles from being dislodged, he stealthily approached the roof's peak. He knew this rooftop, and all the rest in the *pueblo*, like no other man could, but tonight he was being especially careful. Zorro had a dangerous gambit to play—a man would live or die depending on its success. And Zorro meant to succeed.

Before him finally lay the courtyard. Below and directly ahead were the gallows. He was perhaps some fifty feet from the crossbeam from which dangled the noose. The loop of rope was knotted firmly at the end of the crossbeam. That left exposed a six-inch vertical stripe of half-inch–thick rope.

Zorro frowned. What he was planning would take near superhuman precision. But he had practiced. He would not fail.

Scanning the crowd, he noticed only a minimum of soldiers in evidence, proof at least that Yuri's ploy had worked. Neither Gutierrez nor Monastario believed Zorro would appear to rescue the Cossack. On the periphery of the crowd, Zorro spied Bernardo. The servant judiciously avoided glancing in his direction, though he knew exactly where Zorro was hidden. Instead, he stood near the gallows examining them out of the corner of his eye. Zorro followed his gaze, which was now fixed on the trap door. Below was the space into which Yuri's body was meant to drop. Living, if things went according to plan.

There was a slight commotion as Monastario appeared, flanked by Sergeant Garcia and Private Gutierrez. Behind them, two guards led the shackled prisoner up the stairs of the gallows. As the guards placed the Cossack behind the noose, Monastario approached the edge of the platform.

As if he were about to inaugurate a festive occasion, Monastario waved for silence, then began to address the waiting crowd.

"Halt!" Washi called out, raising his hand. The other three Dragon Riders reined their horses.

"We strike them at their heart tonight," he said in Japanese. "Are we prepared?"

Miko nodded curtly as she prepared to don her helmet. Baku bobbed his head brightly. Tanuki frowned; he would wear no mask tonight, having lost his in the previous raid.

"What have you to say?" Washi asked, riding up to him.

"Are we not *ronin*?" Tanuki asked defiantly. "Why do you allow us to submit to him?"

The tall rider faced his younger counterpart.

"We are *ronin,* boy," he said patiently. "Cazador is not our master, but we *do* have an obligation."

Tanuki spat as if the word was rotten piece of fruit in his mouth. "Obligation? To what? Serve as his hell-hounds because of a personal vendetta? You were a nobleman, Washi. You are still noble. Yet you seem more willing to protect the pathetic citizens of this dusty world than your own samurai against an evil man such as Cazador."

Washi laid his hand on the shoulder of the younger man, who pulled back angrily. "Soon this Zorro will appear. And once we bring him to Cazador, we will be free."

Tanuki was silent for a moment. "Free?" he asked sullenly. "To what end?"

"To discover if this new land needs us in the ways Japan used to, now that it has turned its back on us."

"That is all beside the point," Baku, who rarely spoke, said suddenly. He rode up beside Tanuki. Lifting the face of his mask, the musician revealed a broad, lazy grin. "We can kill this time, young one. The false priest commands it."

Washi gave the musician a sharp glare, but all Baku did was broaden his smile affably and turn away. He was correct. Cazador had commanded that they show no mercy in their attack on the *pueblo* tonight. He wanted the samurai free to act as their instincts lead them. And Zorro would be compelled to protect the *pobladores* from the slaughter. The samurai leader could not disagree with the Aztec and maintain control of the *ronin*. So, he put up only the most token resistance, hoping to convince the others outside of Cazador's presence that killing was still unnecessary. The euphoric look on Tanuki's face told Washi that this was not to be.

"I am prepared to strike at their heart. As many hearts as my blades will find!" With that, the boy started to gallop away.

Washi stayed frozen atop his horse for a moment. Shaking his head sadly, he donned his helmet, transforming him into the fearsome monster. Turning, he spurred his horse to catch up with the young soldier. Miko and Baku followed closely behind.

Tonight, it could not be avoided: there would be bloodshed.

"There has been bloodshed!" began Monastario. The crowd murmured among themselves in the dramatic pause that followed. "Many of you, and your loved ones, have suffered at the hands of this man"—he gestured behind him at the prisoner"—and his villainous comrades. . . ."

And on he spoke. Zorro was thankful for the *commandante*'s long-windedness. As the crowd remained alternately enthralled and bored with Monastario's flowery words, Zorro withdrew one of several *kunai* he had brought to the roof. The remainder of the deadly Japanese treasure were stored in packs at Tornado's sides, but these exotic daggers would serve his current purpose.

Taking a knife in hand, Zorro spied the loop of rope over the end of the crossbeam. Narrowing his eyes in concentration, his mind created a tangible line leading from his hand to that rope. There could be no deviation from this line. *I cannot* hope *to strike* that spot, he meditated silently, but the rope must *draw* the blade to it. After repeating the mantra in his mind, Zorro summoned all his skills and threw the *kunai* across the courtyard. He watched it, practically forced it, to travel the line drawn by his mind.

Monastario paused briefly during his speech as the small dagger struck the crossbeam. He tilted his head ever so slightly, then dismissed the noise and continued. He was ranting about invaders to the King's land.

Looking carefully at the gallows, Zorro saw that he had succeeded: the *kunai* had bitten through a section of the rope as it had sunk into the wood of the crossbeam. But the job was only half done. He would have to duplicate the same trick. And quickly, for Monastario's speech was winding down.

Summoning the same absolute concentration, drawing the same mental line from his hand to the crossbeam, Zorro threw the second blade. The *kunai* shot across the courtyard and found its mark.

"What *is* that?", Monastario interrupted himself to say. Garcia and Gutierrez just shrugged. Neither had heard anything—Garcia had been daydreaming of the beer he'd drink tonight, Gutierrez lulled into a fog by his uncle's droning.

"No matter," Monastario continued. He resumed addressing the crowd. "And now I read to you the charges: for crimes against the people of El Pueblo de Los Angeles, and crimes directed ultimately against the King of Spain himself, I, as *commandante* of the *cuartel* of this *pueblo*, sentence this prisoner to be hanged until dead."

Strangely, a smattering of applause rose from the crowd. Monastario began to bow instinctively, then caught himself and stopped. He directed the two guards to lead the prisoner forward. One centered him on the trapdoor while the other draped the noose over the condemned man's head, tightening it around his neck. Finally, from behind the platform, a heretofore unnoticed figure emerged: the hangman.

At the sight of this man, respected and feared like the Grim Reaper himself, the crowd went silent. He gazed at them through a black mask. Many turned away rather than look into his eyes; to do so was considered very bad luck. With the solemnity of a priest about to deliver a benediction, the hangman approached the lever that would release the trap door, killing the prisoner.

Yuri appeared to Zorro as stone-faced as ever. He wondered if even now the Cossack could sense his presence. If so, the man gave no sign. He also gave no indication he would explode in the type of fury he had exhibited in the cantina. The man meant to die.

But Zorro intended otherwise.

The crowd watched with rapt attention at the hanging ritual. Monastario favored them with a grave glance, then turned to the hangman. Not actually looking at the hangman—he was as superstitious as the peasants in this regard—the *commandante* nodded for the lever to be pulled. The hangman did as he was directed. With an audible *ka-chung*, a spring released the trap door beneath the Yuri's feet. He started to fall, but stopped short, caught by the rope around his neck. Choking, but not struggling, the Cossack hung there. Tension on the rope caused him to twist in a counter-clockwise direction, like a leaf hanging from a spiderweb.

And still he choked.

Zorro lifted himself up in alarm. The rope was meant to break, cutting itself on the sharp edges of the dagger blades. Looking more closely, he discovered to his dismay that the second *kunai* had missed the rope by a fraction of an inch. As he expected, the first blade had not been enough to cut the rope on its own, even with the great weight of the Cossack to help things along. Yuri was lucky the initial fall hadn't broken his neck.

But he would die anyway unless Zorro acted quickly, withdrawing a third and final dagger. There was no time for concentration. Only prayer. This was his—and Yuri's—last chance, last hope. Zorro threw the *kunai*.

He did not see the dagger strike the gallows, though the familiar sound told him his aim was true. As soon as he had released the *kunai*, his hands had gone to two pouches tied to his belt. Striking flint, he set them alight. As expected, thick smoke billowed from the burning pouches, which he lobbed into the crowd.

Just then, a loud snap came from the gallows stage. Fearing the worst, Zorro peered down. In the failing light, he saw that his final dagger had cut through the already weakened rope. It broke and Cossack's body plummeted downward, out of sight through the trap door. By now, smoke had started to rise from among the crowd, starting a panic.

Pandemonium broke out. Nerves wound taut from the scene of the execution snapped as violently as the hangman's rope. The screaming started.

Monastario and the others stood up on the stage and begged for calm. The hangman, seemingly oblivious, approached the trap door and peered down. At the edge of the stage, Zorro could see Bernardo lurking. If the final *kunai* had severed the rope in time, Bernardo could use the panic to help the Cossack escape.

Except for the miscalculation in severing the rope, everything had gone according to plan. Everyone in the square seemed convinced that the Dragon Riders were attacking again. Later investigation would find the *kunai* embedded in the gallows, supporting that notion. Zorro's reputation would remain intact. He just hoped the diversion gave Yuri—if he were alive— time to escape.

Already, the panic was subsiding. Despite the momentary confusion, no Dragon Riders had appeared. Men beat at the burning pouches to snuff the flames. As Zorro had hoped, a small dose of chaos went a long way. Time to discover whether his goal of saving Yuri had been reached.

Before he could descend from the roof, Zorro heard something strange. A melody played on a flute-like instrument. He had never heard it, but he knew its meaning well by now. So did the crowd in the square.

"*Madre de Dios*!" someone cried. "It is the Dragon Riders!"

With that, four entrances to the courtyard exploded into fire and thick smoke. Through them rode the Dragon Riders on their ebony horses. Three held blades—one short, one long—in each hand. The feather-maned dragon was armed with a bow. They stopped for a moment, allowing the crowd to see them framed in a billowing inferno. The feathered Dragon Rider drew back on the bowstring and released. This time, it was not a horse that dropped dead. The hangman, grasping the arrow that protruded from his chest, fell lifeless through the trap door and disappeared. So the killing would begin tonight.

As if in response, the tall rider barked an order in his foreign tongue and plunged forward into the crowd on horseback. The others followed suit. All four used their weapons savagely, cutting down anyone in their path.

Many people would die if Zorro did not act quickly.

Chapter 11

No longer worried about concealing himself, Zorro sprang to his feet. Racing along the edge of the tiled roof, he reached the edge and leapt to the next building. This brought him to the corner of the square and behind the feather-maned Dragon Rider.

Diving from the roof, his cape billowing around him like wings, Zorro was a dark blur in the twilight. He struck the Dragon Rider at the waist, knocking the bandit from his horse. The momentum carried both to the ground, Zorro breaking his fall with the Rider's body. The samurai's armor, however, denied him a soft landing.

Below him, the Dragon Rider did not stir. The impact had knocked him unconscious.

"Let's see who we have here," Zorro said to himself, and he rolled the Dragon Rider over on his back. Remembering the construction of the helmet described by Arcadia Flores, he flipped the catch and unmasked the Rider he had felled.

Glossy black hair, as full as the feathered mane, blossomed from within. This rider was a woman. Her beauty struck him even in the dying light. Delicate features, like the portrait of the woman from the Japanese screens, but brought to life in a way that seemed impossible.

What to do about a woman so beautiful, and yet so dangerous?

A harsh yell interrupted his thoughts. His hesitation allowed him to be spotted by the other Riders. Zorro stood as he witnessed a curious thing: the other Dragon Riders' abandoned their attack on the citizens entirely. He suddenly became the magnet to which they were all drawn.

Zorro understood immediately. The others were never the targets of the Riders' attacks. The *ronin* had been waiting for the moment when The Fox would appear. And now that he had, their strange skills and sharp blades would be for him and him alone.

Even now, the Dragon Riders urged their horses through the roiling crowd directly toward him and their fallen comrade. Zorro could spy an excited gleam in the eye of the rider who had been unmasked during the attack on the marketplace. Yes, they all had been waiting very anxiously.

Leaving the fallen rider where she lay, Zorro retreated toward the grandstand, seeing an advantage in higher ground. Springing up to the platform, he could observe the square more clearly. The leader and the unmasked Rider rode toward him from the northwest. Another rider, with a club strapped to his back, approached from the east.

Zorro gave a brief glance down at the trap door of

the gallows. Through the dark opening, he could just make out the form of the murdered hangman. Of the Cossack, there was no sign. Zorro could only hope that Yuri was alive and had escaped. For the moment, he had his own life to worry about.

The crowd was slowing the two Riders to the northwest, but the other was almost upon him. He would have to disable this one, before the contest became three against one.

"Now I have you!" cried a voice behind him.

Zorro whirled toward the voice. Gutierrez, who had never left the stage, stood holding a flintlock. Beside him, saying nothing, was Monastario. Sergeant Garcia's head jerked nervously from the lancer's gun, to Zorro, to the approaching Riders and back again. Soon he would make himself dizzy and swoon, Zorro thought.

"Don't you think you should be pointing that at the Dragon Riders, private?" Zorro asked quickly. He had little time to fuss with Gutierrez, but little choice, either.

"Oh, you mean your accomplices? A clever show, but they'll cease their attack when they see you at my mercy." He stepped forward once more. "And now—"

Gutierrez interrupted himself with a pained yelp as the gun dropped from his hand. In its place protruded the hilt of a small dagger that had been thrown by the Dragon Rider. With deadly accuracy, the blade had been driven completely through the lancer's hand. Gutierrez dropped to his knees in agony.

Zorro turned toward the *ronin* known as the laughing dragon, who was now drawing his club.

Turning back to Gutierrez, Zorro hissed. "If only the strong survive, you are a glaring exception to the rule." The wounded lancer looked up just as he pulled the dagger from his palm. "Remember the next time we meet that I have saved your life." With that, he kicked—pushed, really—Gutierrez from the stage. The soldier fell to the ground and out of harm's way, leaving the blood-coated dagger behind. Zorro turned to confront his enemy, but nuisances on the stage seemed to abound.

"Shoot them both!" Monastario commanded as he drew his gun. Garcia fumbled with his.

In a flash, Zorro's whip lashed out like a living thing at Monastario. The cord encircled the *commandante*'s wrist. A tug dislodged the gun from his hand and Monastario lurched off balance. Another snap, and the whip was cleanly withdrawn. Monastario meanwhile fell yelling into the trap door beneath the gallows. A horrified scream indicated he had encountered a soft landing—on the body of the hangman.

The laughing dragon didn't move, entertained by the prelude to their battle.

"Sergeant Garcia," Zorro said gravely. "You may wish to help your *commandante* at this time. And take care, otherwise, you might fall in yourself and be prevented from fighting both me and our lethal friend here."

The frightened sergeant took his meaning instantly. "Yes, I must help my *commandante*!" Garcia blubbered and immediately fell to edge of the trap door. "Are you all right, *commandante*?" That was all the pretense he offered. Garcia tumbled deliberately through the trap door to safety. A muffled "oof" was heard as the bulky soldier landed on Monastario.

Now only Zorro and the Rider remained. The samurai bowed curtly and presented his club. Zorro drew his sword.

With a cry, the Dragon Rider leapt at Zorro, who quickly sidestepped the charge. Before the *ronin* could recover, the masked man kicked backwards, striking the Dragon Rider behind the knee. The Rider collapsed onto the stage near to where Gutierrez had stood, within reach of the dagger. The blade was in the *ronin*'s hand in a moment—and flying at Zorro in the next. Zorro skillfully deflected the dagger with his sword, but this gave the Dragon Rider time enough to recover. Swinging his great club across the floor of the stage, he knocked Zorro's feet out from under him. He landed on his back, momentarily stunned. The laughing dragon raised the club to attack. Zorro rolled to the side just in time, and the weapon struck the wooden platform only inches from his head.

Dropping his sword for a moment, Zorro quickly grasped the club with both hands and pulled. As he expected, the Dragon Rider would not readily give up his weapon. With all his might, Zorro pulled the Rider toward him, raised his legs and planted his feet on the Dragon Rider's chest. Rolling backwards on his shoulders, Zorro used the *ronin's* own momentum to hurl him from the stage.

Grasping his sword again, Zorro sprang to his feet. The Rider had landed painfully and writhed in agony. Zorro was about to descend from the stage when he sensed motion behind him and spun.

The other two Dragon Riders had reached the stage.

The leader stood his ground with regal authority. The one without the mask was clearly still a boy. He grinned like a cat stalking a canary. The lead Dragon Rider held a spear before him—similarly, the boy brandished a polearm. The curved blade at its end looked as lethal as any sword.

Zorro kept his gaze on the Dragon Riders. The three combatants were alone on the stage. Around them, he was aware of a certain hush that had fallen over the square. Understanding they were out of danger, at least for now, the crowd had stilled, ready to watch the coming battle.

The Dragon Riders stepped forward, spinning the weapons in their hands like deadly propellers.

At first, Zorro advanced with his sword, but the length of their weapons kept him at bay. One aiming high, the other low, only an incredible feat of contortion saved Zorro from being impaled twice.

The leader landed the first blow. The handle of his spear struck Zorro on the side of the head. From the other side, the flat blade of the boy's polearm pierced a section of his cape. At first, Zorro was thankful for the cape, which often caused foes to misjudge the exact position of his body, saving him many a sword and bullet wound. But the boy did not retrieve the polearm for another strike. By the time Zorro understood what was happening, it was too late.

The young Dragon Rider lifted his polearm and began to twirl the cape around it. It caught on Zorro's neck and tightened. Then the boy drove polearm into the stage, anchoring the cape, and immobilizing Zorro. Only a moment was needed to detach the cape, but even this was more time than the leader appeared to need.

The *ronin* jabbed his spear at Zorro, who was pinned in place. His attempt to parry the attack was only partially successful. The Dragon Rider's blade sliced through his shirt on his left side, grazing his ribs and drawing blood.

Ignoring the pain, Zorro freed himself from the cape and twisted one end of it around the lead Dragon Rider's head. He then struck the other man in the stomach, knocking the wind out of him, and tangled him further in the torn cape. This wouldn't hold the *ronin* for long, but perhaps long enough to deal with the younger Dragon Rider. Sword drawn, he face the boy, who now held a slightly curved sword. Their two blades clashed, again and again. For a moment, Zorro was back in his element—a clean swordfight.

Then the boy managed to strike Zorro's sword away from his body, leaving his chest unguarded. Instead of stabbing him, the samurai leapt straight up, delivering a savage flying kick to his face. As Zorro hit the wooden stage, his sword clattered away.

The lead Dragon Rider had untangled himself from the cape and now joined the younger one. Zorro rolled to his left, seizing the polearm still buried in the stage. As the others brought their swords down, he dislodged the polearm, sweeping it before the deadly blades and knocking them aside.

Then he was on his feet again, brandishing the young *ronin*'s original weapon. Hiding his exhaustion, he cracked his trademark smile.

"Please correct me if I start to use this weapon improperly," he jibed. The boy clearly had no idea what he had said and the leader's mask was stone-faced. They raised their swords. Zorro prepared to counter with the polearm.

Just then someone shouted from behind the Dragon Riders. Without turning, the *ronin* each dove aside. Looking beyond where they had stood, Zorro saw the woman he had tackled earlier. He barely saw the blur.

But he felt the pain as something sharp struck his left shoulder.

Jolted backwards, one hand went immediately to the arrow that protruded from his left shoulder. The pain was intense—the wound burned curiously. Poison? Zorro staggered and fell to his knees.

The Dragon Riders on the stage had rolled to a standing position and now approached. Zorro tried to raise himself in defense, but pain and a curious feeling of dislocation caused him to fall back helplessly. They now stood above him, watching him with what appeared to be great curiosity. Their images swam as if through desert heat. A great weight began to settle in his limbs.

The laughing Dragon Rider, the one he had thrown from the platform, now appeared. He stood at Zorro's head, and appeared to be upside-down. Then another shape entered his vision—the woman. The leader and the young rider clapped her on the back in congratulation.

From what he could see of her expression, she seemed loath to accept praise. Her brow knitted in concern. No longer feeling the wound on his shoulder, he reached up with the absurd intention of consoling her.

"It was a fair fight, my lady," he wanted to tell her—even though, in truth, the odds had not at all been fair. It was her beauty that, despite his injury, the pain, and the paralysis that swept through his body, made him want to put her at ease.

Absurd, he realized in his last waking moments. Does one pet a rattlesnake to comfort it? She was no snake though, he thought, his mind meandering. She was a dragon. Even more absently, Zorro wondered if dragons were related to snakes, and if they were poisonous?

Then the black tide overcame him.

Chapter 12

With Zorro vanquished, the Dragon Riders left the square. Their black-clad opponent was slung over the back of Washi's horse. The greatest danger they faced leaving the *pueblo* came not from the military, but from the simple peasants who witnessed their hero being struck down. They swarmed the Dragon Riders, at first heedless of the obvious danger. Still, the peasants were driven away, their bare fists and rocks no match for the swords of the *ronin*.

As they rode into the night, Washi reflected on the show of devotion. The previous nights' brutalities had been forgotten by those who loved and respected this Fox. Doubtless, Zorro was, in his way, a samurai. In another time, he would be their ally.

But these were not those times. And honor meant fulfilling promises. And the sooner they fulfilled their promise to Cazador, the sooner this would all end, and a new life could truly begin.

Certainly the old life was over. The courts, the emperors, the elite squads of samurai were all things of the past. The samurai were now expected to become bureaucrats. The code of the *bushido* had become meaningless in the current state of affairs.

Washi had tried to adapt. The feudal lord he had served became a successful governor; so, Washi traded his *katana* for a quill pen, helping supervise the region's affairs, becoming an *attaché*. The velvet clothes of a courtier were certainly much more comfortable than the lacquered wood armor of a samurai, but he was otherwise completely unsuited to a life of bookkeeping, administration and the entertainment of softbodied dignitaries.

And so, as did many others like him who yearned for the old ways, the ways of honor, the code of the *bushido*—the Way of the Warrior—he broke with his former master and returned to the life of the samurai. But those who followed *bushido* became *ronin*. They followed the wave of changes in the land, riding before them, remaining a constant force amid the chaos. But it made them outlaws in their own land. Certainly, their services were for hire, when it suited some individual's purpose. But where they were not welcome, they were criminals.

Washi found it ironic that to escape their lot in the changing Japan, they had sold themselves to become criminals in this new land. Still, there was something to be said for having a purpose finally. A purpose to be fulfilled with battle and blade and blood.

Baku smiled lazily to himself, as he was often found doing. He was not thinking of the previous battle. Or even the music he enjoyed playing. The stars crowding the desert sky held no enchantment for him.

No, he was envying *kitsune,* Zorro, and where the man must be right now. Certainly, his body was in sight, on Washi's horse, and the masked man was alive; but he was not *with them,* in a greater sense. Zorro was somewhere else, somewhere deep inside himself, yet far outside this universe. Miko's arrow had been coated with a powerful dose of a mescaline mixture that combined both his own skills and those of Hidalgo el Cazador. From his own experience, Baku knew the substance coursing through The Fox's veins was transporting him to realms unimaginable.

Perhaps when Cazador was appeased, Baku himself would follow in The Fox's tracks.

The thought of such a journey made him think of his *shakuhachi.* His elegant flute, his dangerous weapon. The slightest frown clouded his expression when he remembered that the battle with Zorro had put it in some disrepair. It would be out of tune if he tried to play it now. But this shade of discontent faded quickly. Baku was smiling lightly to himself once more.

At Tanuki's age, which had not been so long ago, he had been wild also. Even more wild, and considered too undisciplined by many. And so, he was sent to live among the Buddhist priests of the Fukeshu sect. There, he was schooled in spiritual matters in order to calm him and help him find self control. Students were taught to meditate to the music of the *shakuhachi* rather than using the standard chants of Zen Buddhism.

As in all things before, Baku rebelled at first. Then he made several discoveries that transformed his life.

He soon found the music of the flute to be soothing and calming. Around the same time, he discovered the herbs that, especially when combined with the ethereal tones of the flute, produced the empty, beatific smile on his face.

The *shakuhachi* was 1.8 feet long, slightly less than the length of a *katana*. It was made this way because swords were forbidden in the company of the Fukeshu priests. Baku was taught to fashion his own flute as part of his studies. He found a distinct bamboo that created a flute capable of producing haunting tones, but also possessed a certain sturdiness, making it suitable as a weapon.

And so he trained, with the flute the focus of his meditation and, secretly, his skills as a warrior. Finally, it came time to leave the priests. By then, of course, Japan had moved on and there was no longer a place for him. The priests would gladly have welcomed him back, but a sedate life of flute-playing held little appeal.

So he set out into the countryside, faring better than most *ronin*—mainly because of his flute. Baku would travel from town to town, raising money by playing music and, in the right situation, earning greater sums of money by wielding the same instrument as a weapon.

Washi had found him at an inn, playing for his room and board. The stately older man had seen his fire, as easily as he had seen that of Tanuki's, which burned brightly. They formed a casual alliance, which became formal when word came of work in a new land called "California."

Wandering across the ocean seemed like a grand adventure of the kind he had only experienced in his mind, so he readily agreed. His plan, of course, was to return to solitary wandering after delivering Zorro to Cazador. At the moment, he was experiencing too much companionship. But at least things had been interesting.

A muffled moan rose from Zorro. Baku's smile widened almost imperceptibly.

Where are you now, kitsune? Baku asked in his mind. *I'd join you when our work is done, but then, when our work is done, the only place I could join you is in death. And that's not the adventure I planned.*

Baku glanced back at Miko, who was lost in her own thoughts. He had tipped two arrows with the powerful drug, and she had used only one to fell Zorro. Would Miko pass him the arrow if he asked? It was a long trip and, without his flute to play, he could use another distraction. But no matter. There was plenty more at the hidden city; Cazador had promised.

Certain they were not being pursued, Washi slowed their pace. Excited by their victory over The Fox, and the scent of their impending freedom from Cazador heavy in his nostrils, Tanuki wanted to fly into the night at a full gallop. The fight with Zorro had energized him greatly. Finally, an opponent of skill, not some poor peasant desperately defending his home. There had been some sport, and true spirit, in their confrontation. His only regret was that Miko's tainted arrow had ended the battle. He had known, they had all known, that Zorro was to be captured, not killed. But once again, Tanuki felt robbed by the Aztec priest. A man like Zorro, were he to die, was meant to die with honor in battle, not to be put to death while drugged and defenseless.

Ah, but who knew of honor in these lands? And who had been tempered in the fires of battle? No one, by his observation, except the fox they had trapped. The soldiers they had seen were weak, the people dull and downtrodden. After Zorro, there would be no sport, no spirit.

This spirit had first torn loose from Japan with the disbanding of the samurai. It briefly knitted together the *ronin* who insisted on following the *bushido,* but in a weakened form. Once revered as fierce and loyal warriors, they were now cast as dangerous criminals, adherents to a violent and uncivilized history that a new country wished to forget. The bureaucrats had legislated the spirit from Japan. Tanuki had joined with Washi, in whom he had seen glimpses of that spirit, to try this new land. They had hoped to reclaim the spirit here. But the only sign that the spirit existed lay unconscious on the back of their leader's horse.

To have seen Zorro's skill at battling multiple opponents as he had, to have witnessed his confident and devilish smile despite his obvious exhaustion, was to know that their search had not been entirely in vain. But The Fox's end would not be fitting, of this Tanuki was certain. And the spirit would elude them once more.

"We must stop," Miko said suddenly, pulling up along side Washi. He slowed further, but did not stop entirely. They were in the foothills now, about to begin the arduous ascent to Cazador's hidden city.

"Cazador awaits, Miko," Washi said gently. "And the sooner we deliver Zorro to him, the sooner we can be rid of them both."

"Agreed," she replied. "But perhaps I should treat the prisoner's wounds. The rest of the journey is difficult, and the priest wants Zorro brought to him alive."

Washi now halted his stallion and considered.

"Even a man such as Cazador may wait for his prize," Miko ventured boldly. "We have Zorro. Whether it is tonight or in the morning, Cazador will get what he wants."

"We camp," Washi said simply. "Baku, prepare a fire. Tanuki, help me with the prisoner so that Miko may attend to him."

As they all dismounted, Miko said a silent prayer of thanks. She could use a few more hours away from Cazador's lethal gaze. And to consider the problem of the *kitsune*. Indeed, she was now convinced that the spirit of the fox resided in the man they called Zorro.

Soon, water was boiling over a fire made of desert deadwood. Miko removed Zorro's shirt to examine his shoulder and ribs. The Fox's strong torso distracted her from her task. Her eyes were continually drawn to his chest, which rose and fell with shallow breathing, and in particular to the pulsating spot where his heart beat. The firelight seemed to glow from within his skin rather than shine on its surface. She looked at his face, and even reached for his mask. *What would he look like underneath?* she wondered. During their struggle, their eyes had met. Even closed they seemed to sparkle. The set of his lips remained sensual.

She withdrew her hand from his mask. To reveal him this way would bring dishonor on them both. She felt an unexpected blush of shame for even having removed his shirt, though it had been necessary for her to examine his wound.

With effort, she redirected her attention to his wounded shoulder. Zorro had twisted slightly to the side as the arrow struck him, causing only a crease in his flesh. Still, the drug had quickly worked its way into his system.

The wounds cleaned and dried, Miko bandaged Zorro's shoulder and chest. Before replacing his shirt, she placed her hand over his heart. His skin was warm, as if the fire truly did burn from within, and his heart was strong. Very strong. This man was powerful. It almost frightened her.

"Laying on hands to heal, priestess?" came a sudden voice. Miko reflexively jerked her hand back and looked up. Baku stood above her, a lascivious taint to his usual wide grin. "I have a few bruises from our battle I'd like you to look at when you're done with the prisoner. I promise to make a more responsive patient."

While his insinuations shamed Miko, she nonetheless would not tolerate them. Barely shifting her weight, she lashed out with one foot, sweeping Baku's legs out from under him. He fell to the ground heavily. The smile never left his face.

"Perhaps not," he said with the same blithe cheer, rolled to a standing position and walked away.

The Dragon Riders prepared to bed down for the night. At Washi's instructions, Tanuki bound Zorro's hands and feet. He was also directed to keep first watch on the prisoner while the others slept. Baku had fixed his flute and played a lilting melody before turning in himself.

The music masked the sound of an approaching horse, which ceased soon after the rider saw the fire the *ronin* had built, a flickering beacon across the dark plain. Dismounting, the mysterious rider led the horse as quietly as possible in a roundabout way towards the Dragon Riders' encampment.

Chapter 13

The desert sands flowed and shifted, the colors of the twilight sky—deep blue, gold, shimmering pink, and more. It was hard to tell where the desert stopped and the sky began.

Except for the stars. They twinkled above. The scene was calm, peaceful, the wind a gentle caress on Zorro's cheeks.

Movement above. Four stars, detaching themselves from the heavens. Descending, slowly at first. Floating down to earth.

The idyll ended.

The wind picked up instantly, quickly rising to a howl. Sand whipped his face, stung his cheeks. The gentle hues of sunset drained from everything, leaving sky and earth the crimson color of blood. The four stars—now four fireballs—rushed earthward, heading straight for him. Bright bursts lit the sky as they struck the atmosphere.

Strangely paralyzed, Zorro could only watch the harbingers of his doom approach.

Then they struck, four blazing comets, exploding against the desert before him. He shielded his eyes from the debris that spewed from the impact, but could otherwise not protect himself. Stones and sand pummeled him. But he did not fall. The deafening roar of the wind suddenly ceased. The cooling earth hissed and crackled.

Lowering his arm revealed an ominous sight: four gallows, each rising from a smoking crater, the sand around them blasted into a moat of black glass. The four fingers of rock formed the claw of a great beast threatening to drag Zorro beneath the desert floor. Their surfaces, cratered and glowing like the moon, would have made them unrecognizable as gallows save for the familiar ropes dangling from each crooked fingertip.

The fingers appeared to beckon, ending his paralysis as he was drawn toward the gallows. A hiss from above halted him. As if by magic, four bat-winged forms now appeared, each perched on a rocky finger like a gargoyle.

But these were not gargoyles. They were dragons.

The largest one hissed again at Zorro.

"Live an extraordinary life, little fox, and others will die extraordinary deaths."

In the blink of an eye, a hooded figure appeared on each platform before him. One by one, a vile creature reached down, unmasking each victim. In turn, each pale, trembling face was revealed, framed by the noose dangling before it: his father, Bernardo, Arcadia Flores and Yuri.

"It is an irony as sharp as the sword you wield. Live peacefully, ordinarily, and so do others. Fight for justice, battle evil—and evil will seek those you love." The creature hissed once more. "Is your justice worth the cost?"

The dragon sat above his father, whom he now pushed forward, his neck encircled by the noose.

"What is this, Diego? What have you brought upon us?" his father cried as the dragon drew the cord tight against his neck.

Zorro preferred death to witnessing the pale, frightened expression on his father's face. Worse still was Bernardo's disapproving expression. Unable to speak, he radiated disgust at Zorro for having brought them all to this ignoble end. The dragon pushed him forward through the noose and tightened it like a tie on a small child.

Tears flowed down Arcadia's face as she was urged to step forward. The dragon took a moment to stroke the woman's long, silky hair after he had fixed the noose in place. Arcadia pulled away from the monster's touch, only to be stopped short by the noose.

"I thought you had saved us, and I loved you for that," she choked. "But my father and brother are dead, and soon, so shall I be. I curse you, Don Diego de la Vega, as you curse all who cross your path!" Her sadness gave way to rage, and she spit at him.

Yuri stepped forward with no urging. His expression was grim. "You helped me. You condemned me. They are the same things."

"Let them go!" Zorro roared suddenly, no longer able to stand idly by as his loved ones suffer. Unsheathing his sword he prepared to storm the gallows.

The largest dragon gave one flap of his leathery wings and landed directly in front of Zorro. One claw flashed out and grasped Zorro by the neck and pulled him forward. With an evil smile, the creature looked him straight in the eye. Its breath was rank and hot. Steam hissed from its nostrils.

"That's right, little fox, fight. Save your friends." He uttered a laugh that sounded like the screams of a cattle slaughter. "Save them, kill them. Like the man said, they are the same things in the end."

Zorro brought up his sword. The blade bit into the creature's belly and sliced upward. The dragon instantly released his neck and stepped back. It was laughing wetly. Withdrawing his sword, Zorro saw that he had practically gutted the thing—a three foot long incision ran up to its chest. Fire and smoke belched from the wound. Lava began to gush onto the desert floor, sizzling as it struck the ground. Zorro had to step back to avoid being burned.

"They are the same thing!" the beast laughed again.

Zorro looked at his sword, now twisted into a misshapen club by the creature's intense internal heat. Tossing away the useless weapon, he withdrew his whip.

The dragon coughed, spitting a fireball into the air, and fell backwards, expiring. More lava erupted from its body. He heard shrieking—the other dragons were flying at him from the gallows. He raised the whip to attack, no matter the futility. It twitched in his hand, alive. The whip had transformed into a rattlesnake which coiled to strike back at Zorro. He just barely threw it into the inferno of the large dragon in time. Now he was completely unarmed to face his foes.

The other dragons, however, came not for him, but instead descended upon the body of their fallen leader. With fangs and claws, they tore at the dragon in a frenzy.

Zorro sprinted past them to save the others before their bloodlust wore off. He crossed the scorched earth and sprang up to the platform where his father continued to stand.

"It will be all right," he said attempting to loosen the rope around his father's neck. Astoundingly, his father stepped back out of reach.

"No."

"What is this? We have to hurry!" He reached again for his father, who dodged his hands.

"It is the same thing. Save us now and you condemn us to a worse fate to come."

"You're scared—" he began, but Arcadia interrupted him.

"Let us die here," she cried. "It is inevitable. It became inevitable the moment you donned that mask."

"No!" Their words stung him. He had become Zorro only to help, never to harm.

"You made the choice regardless of its consequences," the Cossack intoned, "and we are consequences. As are our deaths."

"No!" He tried to say more, but the reproach in Bernardo's eyes stopped him. He would not be allowed to save them. All his struggles, all his battles, had been for nothing if he could not save those closest to him.

Just then, a great tremor shook the earth. Zorro was nearly thrown from the platform. A roar bellowed behind him and he turned.

At the spot where he had slain the dragon there now boiled a crater of lava. The other dragons threw themselves into it with gleeful abandon. As they did, the earth rumbled again. Despite their words, he had to get the others out of here. Turning back to his father, he found the gallows empty. Don Alejandro was gone. Looking to the other platforms, he saw that Bernardo and the others had also vanished.

There came a great crack and the furthest gallows crumbled. Another shock ruined the next. Zorro leapt from his father's gallows, knowing its destruction was imminent. He faced the lava cauldron. It spread out before him like a fiery pool of blood, bubbling and smoking.

From beneath its surface, a great bulk started to rise. The heat from the lava was so intense, Zorro could not make out the shape at first. Whatever it was, it was larger than the four dragons combined. Soon, Zorro was dwarfed by a creature that rose as high as the bluffs near the *hacienda*.

Wings, which had been folded to protect this creature from the lava, spread wide, nearly obliterating the sky. A great neck uncoiled, lifting an enormous head. Feline eyes gleamed. A mouth large enough to swallow a horse whole leered at Zorro. A great dragon emerged from the pool of lava and towered over him.

"Your friends are dead, little fox," it spoke to him in a deep voice. "They, and all the others you sought to champion."

Zorro turned to escape. Unarmed, the creature was beyond his ability to combat. Perhaps nothing would help him prevail against such a monster, but to face it now was to die. But before he had gone even a step, the dragon reached out with a great wing and batted him effortlessly to the ground. Sand sought Zorro's lungs, choking him. As he rose, the dragon struck again and flipped him onto his back. It loomed over him. Flight was impossible.

"You feed me, little fox," the dragon began. "With each soul you think you save, you serve them up to me. I am all the lies you tell to protect your identity. I am the risks you take to safeguard the ones you love. I am the hatred you generate in those who wish for the natural order, where the strong subjugate the weak. You throw off the balance of nature, little fox. I am the likelihood that one mistake on your part will bring about the doom of anyone you have touched with your unique presence."

The dragon's maw was directly above him now. The heat and smell of its breath were stifling. It would kill him. And by rights, it appeared he deserved it.

"Oh no, I'll not kill you," the creature almost purred, plucking the thoughts from Zorro's brain. "You are flawed in a most spectacular way! Despite my words, you'll continue your crusade, compounding all the lies and the risks, and I'll continue to grow fat and powerful. There would be no sport in killing you now."

The dragon raised his head once more. As it did so, Zorro again noticed the feline slivers of its pupils.

"Go now. And feed me," said the great dragon, dismissing him.

Zorro barely heard its command, captivated as he was by the creature's eyes. Bowing its head, the great dragon folded its wings around itself and began to sink slowly into the lava. On its head, Zorro thought he saw spots dancing just beneath the surface of the dragon's skin. Familiar spots.

The dragon was now partially submerged by the lava. Impulsively, he rose to his feet and ran toward the creature.

"Wait!" he called out. "Stop!"

The dragon's wings ruffled a bit, widening so that

it could peer out at him. It seemed surprised to be interrupted. Zorro could see the spots more clearly now and recognized their pattern: that of a jaguar pelt.

"I said go!" the dragon bellowed.

"You also said to feed you," Zorro answered. He had reached the edge of pool of lava. "So I will."

With that, he used his momentum to leap at the dragon. When it gaped in surprise, Zorro was able to grasp a large tooth. His hands burned from the heat radiating even from the creature's tooth, but he held on, hoisting himself into the dragon's mouth before it could close. Its slimy, forked tongue curled around him like a python.

The dragon gagged, attempting to speak. Zorro held tight to another tooth to avoid being spit out, then dived forward down the thing's throat. If he were wrong, he would die here, in the gullet of this unearthly beast. But the creature talked of risks and had spoken at least one truth: As long as he remained alive, he would not turn from challenges. And this seemed to be a great one indeed.

Fighting his way down against the constricting muscles of the dragon's throat, air became scarce. The temperature rose as he clawed his way to the thing's infernal heart. Zorro intended to rip it out, to tear the heart out of the lies it had uttered.

Around him, he could feel the dragon shuddering, agonized by the damage he was doing. It was attempting to expel him from its body. He would not allow that. If nothing else, the thing would choke on him.

He continued downward. Even in this large beast, space started to close in around him.

Tearing his way through walls of flesh, he entered

the dragon's chest. The malformed organ lay before him, beating in the faint glow of lava. The heart itself was ice-cold to the touch. He wrapped his arms around the dragon's heart, ignoring the new burning sensation of sub-zero temperatures. The frenzied pulsing of the dragon's heart threatened to throw him off. But he held tight, and squeezed tighter. The dragon was dying. The heart weakening. Finally, it beat no more.

The cooling lava in the dragon's veins dimmed the light in the heart chamber. Then the light vanished entirely. Zorro stood in the dark, wondering what would happen next.

With a gasp, Zorro awoke in the Dragon Riders' camp.

Chapter 14

Instinctively, Zorro tried to rise. Both the ropes that bound him and the dull pain in his body dragged him back down again. His vision swam as he stared at the embers of the Dragon Riders' dying fire. The great dragon seemed to rise from their ashes, the next moment, it was merely a fire once more.

Coherent thought was taxing. That he had been struck by a drugged arrow was his first clear memory. Breathing slowly and deeply, he spread his awareness over his body as best he could. His head ached; the least of his worries. He was bound securely at the wrists and ankles. This, he felt, was a real cause for concern.

A dull fire throbbed in his left shoulder, as well as his chest, but nothing more. The image of the beautiful Dragon Rider rose in his mind. He pictured her stance clearly—she had barely given her accomplices time to dive aside before she let the arrow fly. And he had had no time to react. But here he was alive, when she could have easily killed him. Instead, he had been kidnapped. His wounds had been carefully treated.

The Dragon Riders' care in keeping him alive gave him cold comfort. This could only mean that a more terrible fate was in store for Zorro than a quick death—the *ronin* could have provided that. No, the samurai were being directed by another. And Zorro could guess who that was.

Now, he thought, *to the business of escaping, since I don't wish to suffer a fate worse than death. Death is bad enough on its own.*

The *ronin* had tied his hands and feet, but not staked him to the ground. Small victory, he thought grimly. He wouldn't get far just rolling away into the desert.

He turned on his side towards the glowing embers of the campfire. In its steady light, he could see the forms of sleeping *ronin*. At first, the number in their party seemed to have increased. Many dark shapes rested on the ground around the fire, the closest perhaps ten feet away. Focusing through the drug-induced haze that still dulled his senses, he realized that he had mistaken discarded armor for additional samurai. Among the empty shells, three of the *ronin* slept soundly. The fourth, the boy, sat up against a tree. He had fallen asleep while keeping watch, still clad in his armor.

The samurai's swords were too far away for Zorro to consider cutting his bonds with a blade. He weighed other options. The firepit. Slowly, he made his way toward it. Very slowly. The intermittent fog in his brain made the journey interminable. Once, he lost consciousness only to be jolted awake by the pain of his shoulder. Finally, he reached the firepit—the boy sleeping on his watch had not stirred.

Keeping his body low, Zorro stretched his wrists toward a large ember. The heat reminded him of the great dragon again, but he pushed the image away. Lowering his wrists to the ember, Zorro pressed the rope against it. He was grasping the dragon's tooth once more. But as in his nightmare, he persevered, the searing heat scorching his skin as he tried to burn through the rope.

Pretending to be asleep, Tanuki watched Zorro with fascination. He had indeed been dozing, but the prisoner had shouted as he awoke, waking Tanuki as well. How Zorro had emerged from his mescaline trance was beyond the boy's reckoning. The masked man should have been unconscious until well into the next morning. Zorro possessed the most powerful will he had ever witnessed in his young life.

He had almost cheered Zorro on toward the fire. Disappointment when he fell unconscious turned to excitement as Tanuki saw the prisoner claw his way up from the depths of his own mind to resume his struggle. Burning through the ropes seemed like a dangerous proposition, one the young *ronin* was anxious to witness. What would burn more quickly, Zorro's ropes or Zorro himself? The Fox was obviously in pain as he, too, waited for the answer, his wrists thrust into the fire pit. The smell of burning rope—and was that other odor charred flesh?—soon reached Tanuki where he sat.

Abruptly, the prisoner rolled away from the fire. His back was to Tanuki, who almost gave himself away by shifting position to see what had happened.

Smoke, and perhaps a bit of flame, had risen from Zorro's wrists, but they were now obscured by his body. Zorro folded into a fetal position. Had the pain become too much? Had the Fox given in to defeat?

The answer came as Zorro silently rose to his feet, free of the ropes that had bound him. He rubbed his wrists but seemed otherwise uninjured from the ordeal. Still, his eyes seemed unsure of his surroundings. He had not entirely overcome Baku's drug.

But no matter. Tanuki's own goal had been achieved. He had wanted Zorro to escape—or more precisely, to attempt escape. This way, if he had to kill the prisoner to keep him from escaping, he would be justified.

Tanuki dropped his pretense of sleep and rose, his *katana* drawn.

So the boy had been watching him all along, Zorro thought as the samurai approached. He did not attempt to run. He would be caught easily. The expression on the boy's face, pleasure and deadly determination mingling in his eyes, was disquieting. Still, Zorro stood his ground.

"You could have helped," Zorro told him in a whisper as the boy approached.

The samurai acknowledged him only by pressing a finger to his lips. He pointed behind Zorro with his sword. Besides the horses, there were only more foothills in that direction. His eyes never leaving his quarry, the boy went to the tree where the other weapons rested and withdrew a sword similar to his own from a scabbard. He now pointed with both swords, indicating with a nod that Zorro march toward the foothills.

The danger was obvious—he was being led, unarmed, into the desert by a young man holding two swords, and obviously skilled at using both simultaneously. Still, they would be apart from the group, and any advantage he could gain over the boy might allow him to escape.

Zorro only hoped the samurai would not suddenly strike him down as soon as they were out of sight from the rest of the Dragon Riders.

It fleetingly occurred to Zorro to awaken the others, but that would only ensure his recapture. Best to take his chances with this one alone than with all four at the same time, so he complied. Past the horses, Zorro was directed to turn west, where they hiked up a small hill, then back down to a clearing. The two were completely obscured by the hills.

The boy barked a command at him and he turned. What was he after? Zorro wondered. The *ronin* said a few more words that Zorro could not understand, so he just shook his head. Frustrated, the boy thought a moment, then held out the second sword, presenting the hilt. Nodding, he urged Zorro to take it. He did so carefully, never taking his eyes off the samurai.

Stepping back, the boy put his sword through some paces—thrusting, slicing through the air, testing its balance. When through, he turned expectantly to Zorro. With a nod, the boy urged him to do the same. Again, Zorro complied. It was a well-balanced, well-made sword. A fine weapon. Still, whether due to the drug lingering in his system or the strangeness of finding himself at sword practice at a time like this, he felt very unreal. Nodding his approval of the sword, he turned to see what the boy would do next.

The samurai bowed briskly, to which Zorro replied in kind. Then the boy raised his sword and assumed first position for attack.

So that was the game, Zorro quickly realized. A duel. And, he understood something else: they would duel to the death, with only ancient hills and a twisted Joshua tree as their witnesses.

With battle cry, the boy attacked him with the speed of a striking cobra. Even in the *pueblo*, the boy had not exhibited such swiftness. Still, Zorro was certain that, unimpaired by injuries and the drug that coursed through him, he was more than a match for the *ronin*. But his reflexes were slowed and his shoulder stiff. If he were not careful, the boy might very well succeed where others had failed. Still, Zorro could fend off his vigorous attacks, even while giving some ground.

That's when the boy attempted a flying kick as he had on the stage. Having seen the maneuver, Zorro was able to avoid the kick, but managed to throw himself off-balance anyway. The samurai brought his sword down again and again. Fighting for balance, Zorro barely avoided the sword that came slicing at him.

The world swam in and out of focus and Zorro faltered. Thankfully, the boy noticed, ceasing his attack and allowing the spell to pass. Zorro's mind cleared.

And clearly, he would not last much longer. Luckily, the boy had shown his weakness.

Two lightning kicks struck Zorro suddenly—one high and one low. Zorro hit the ground. Summoning all his skills, he parried a lightning series of attacks as he stood. The exertion caused the world to waver before him again.

As before, the young *ronin* waited for his opponent to recover. Though his vision cleared, Zorro feigned continued dizziness. Taking a great chance, he then dropped his sword, staggered drunkenly forward and collapsed. Now Zorro waited.

Approaching warily, the boy nudged him with the toe of his boot. Zorro remained still. Then the *ronin* prodded him in the arm with the tip of his sword, stabbing just deeply enough to draw blood. Zorro made no reaction—he felt only the suggestion of pain. Earlier, as he burned his ropes free, he had discovered that, his shoulder notwithstanding, the drug in his system had numbed his body. When the boy had kicked him during their duel, he heard rather than felt the blows strike his body. As long as the boy didn't attempt to wound him any more seriously, he could convincingly appear to be unconscious.

The charade worked. The boy put away his sword and rolled Zorro onto his back, clearly disappointed that his sport had been ruined. Now he seemed unsure of what to do. Killing Zorro while helpless was clearly unacceptable.

Zorro saved him the trouble by striking the boy in the temple with a rock. He landed on his back, groaning, only semi-conscious.

It would have to do, Zorro thought. No time for tying him. Just time to escape.

Tossing the samurai's sword into the brush, Zorro took one with him and returned to the horses. He risked waking the others, but knew he wouldn't get far without a horse. Luckily, they were tied some thirty yards from where the others slept. He untied all four horses and leapt onto the back of one. His sudden appearance unsettled them, but this served his purposes. Driving his horse forward, he scattered the others. Soon he was at a full gallop. He thought he heard the shouts of the waking Dragon Riders behind him but concentrated only on riding away from them.

Even if they were able to round up the other horses, he would have enough of a head start. They would search for their missing companion before setting off after him in any case.

He had escaped. For the moment, at least.

Chapter 15

As he rode into the night, Zorro realized that the drug made the world around him an alien landscape. He was soon unsure whether he rode toward his hideaway or deeper into the mountains. Often, the moonlit terrain would twist and warp like it had in his nightmare. His consciousness would fold in on itself, threatening to resurrect the great dragon once more.

The great dragon, he knew, had been the malformed product of his own mind, born of the self-doubt that lingered in his soul like a wisp of smoke curling from the creature's muzzle. And though he had slain the dragon in the vision, he knew that it only lay dormant; it waited to rise and be fed once more. Ironically, the memory of Hidalgo el Cazador had helped him defeat the dragon. When its scaly veneer had failed, revealing the jaguar spots beneath, Zorro realized what was happening: he was threatening to fall prey to himself, the most formidable opponent he could imagine.

He doubted Cazador himself was the source of the dragon's manifestation; he had broken the false priest's hold on his mind during their last encounter. But the spots revealed Cazador's hand in the Dragon Riders' actions. Zorro had shown himself that the great dragon was as ephemeral as any shadow of fear cast over him. But a piece of it would remain within him forever and, like any eternal creature, could be resurrected again and again.

The tricky business of being Zorro would provide ample opportunity. The dragon would be fed. As the events of the nightmare had shown, the actions of Zorro, no matter how well-meaning, could cause the persecution of those around him. While keeping his identity secret protected those close to him, the case of the Cossack illustrated that even one who didn't know his identity could be used as bait.

His thoughts returned to the events prior to the Dragon Riders' attack at the execution. Thinking back, Zorro was not certain that he had saved the Cossack's life. The savageness of the Dragon Riders' attack hindered his ability to isolate any clue, any image, from his memory that confirmed that Yuri had escaped.

Realizing he had blacked out, Zorro dragged himself out of the past, through his nightmare, and into the present. Great hills surrounded him. Not far to his right was a sheer cliff face. The mountains had swallowed him. He was lost.

Reining his horse to a halt, he surveyed the land around him. He could hear the beat of hooves in the distance—the Dragon Riders were on the hunt—but remained still. Better to get his bearings and plan his route than to continue to run blindly.

Another sound reached his ears. Water rushing. He could use some water, to refresh his body and to splash onto his face. The noise emanated from over the next rise. Following the cliff face, he urged his horse toward it. Not far, he found a waterfall cascading down from the mountain crags, collecting in a clear pool. Wavelets spread from where the waterfall struck its surface. Moonlight danced in blue, spreading rings.

He didn't realize how thirsty he was until that moment.

Dismounting, he crouched at the bank of the pool. In the dim light, he could see his reflection. A sorry sight, haggard and pale. Cupping his hands he scooped up water to splash on his face. Its icy coolness was such a shock to his system that another wave of dizziness struck and he fell forward into the pool. After a moment of disorientation, Zorro began to thrash. The pool was much deeper than it appeared. He could not quite tell which direction was up. The conviction that, after surviving his many adventures, he would simply drown, alone in the mountains, bubbled up to the surface of his tumult-filled mind.

Suddenly, a strong hand grasped his arm. He was wrenched upward and out of the water, then unceremoniously deposited on the sandy bank of the pool. Coughing, he ejected water from his lungs, blinking to clear his vision. When his sight returned, he found himself staring up into the eyes of Yuri. The Cossack's demeanor was as grim as ever.

But even that was not the greatest surprise. What brought Zorro leaping to his feet at the risk of swooning again was the sight of his grand, black stallion standing beside the horse he had taken from the Dragon Riders.

"Tornado!" he cried, and at his voice, the horse ambled toward him and whickered in recognition. "How . . . ?" he began as he stroked Tornado's muzzle, turning back to the Cossack, who watched the reunion in silence.

"Hurry," he said simply and leapt skillfully onto Tornado's back. Zorro tensed, expecting to have to dodge the Cossack's huge body as the horse ejected him from the saddle. Instead, Yuri simply offered his hand so that Zorro could mount Tornado, who stood perfectly calm. He was almost too shocked to move, and the Cossack nearly yanked his arm from his socket pulling him up. Fleetingly, Zorro thought that perhaps he was still drowning, and that this was a new type of vision conjured by the drug.

"Yah!" The Cossack suddenly shouted in a fearsome roar that frightened the Dragon Rider's horse. Whinnying in fear, it galloped wildly away. They took a moment to watch it go, then the two men rode away on Tornado in a different direction.

Sitting astride Tornado behind Yuri, Zorro could see a livid burn encircling the man's neck. The noose had bitten into the Cossack's flesh before the rope had snapped. Similar burns surrounded the man's wrists where he had been bound. Even though Yuri was alive, Zorro was nonetheless shamed that the man had come to this much harm. Within him, the great dragon opened one feline eye and exhaled a wisp of acrid smoke.

"What happened?" Zorro asked in Russian. He had other questions, but they all boiled down to that one.

"*Muchas cosas*," Yuri answered in Spanish. "Many.

things." He did not look back to gauge Zorro's reaction—which was great surprise.

"Please explain—" Zorro began, but the Cossack
held up a hand to silence him.

"In time."

And so Zorro held his tongue and his questions.
The Cossack would explain in his own time, obviously. Surprisingly, they were not heading back toward Los Angeles, but instead plunging deeper into
the mountains. Soon, a black hole appeared in a
mountain face above them. A cave.

So the Cossack had a hiding place as well, Zorro
thought. No wonder he had disappeared from the
Mission. The Dragon Riders had been taking Zorro
up the mountains as well, no doubt where Cazador
was now located. Cave dwellings seemed as common
as adobe huts here in the mountains, he thought
dryly.

Yuri halted Tornado just below the mouth of the
cave and both dismounted. Throwing Tornado's
leather packs over his shoulder, the Cossack motioned
for Zorro to follow. Together they ascended a steep,
thirty-foot incline. The large man walked with confidence, as if he were simply strolling across a ballroom
floor. Zorro, however, weak and exhausted, used the
gnarled desert plants that dotted their path to haul
himself arduously upward. A misstep dislodged a
stone, causing it to roll from underfoot in a small av-
alanche of pebbles and dirt. He backslid briefly, nearly
tumbling backwards. Yuri simply glanced back, saw
that Zorro himself had not become part of a landslide,
and continued his effortless climb.

Finally, they reached the mouth of the cave, both
needing to stoop before its low ceiling. Several feet in,
the rock rose sharply above them, allowing even the

giant Cossack to stand at full height. The moonlight seemingly afraid to follow them, the cave interior was pitch black. As easily as he had climbed the steep hill, Yuri plunged into the darkness and was swallowed whole. His heavy but quick footsteps shuffled away. Moving cautiously, Zorro dragged a hand lightly against the cool stone wall to his left. After the sound of flint scraping on stone, light flared suddenly at the far end of the cave. A small candle glowed with just enough light to allow them to see, but not enough to reach the mouth of the cave itself. Their location would not be revealed.

Zorro could now make out the cave's details. About forty feet deep, the cave never became wider than four men walking abreast, or higher than a few feet over the Cossack's head. Packed dirt and stone made up the floor, which was mostly level. In all, the cave appeared to be a fingerhole poked by a massive giant.

The Cossack had carefully removed all loose stones from the cave, leaving only two large boulders for use as rudimentary chairs. A rough mat of straw marked where he slept. Other paltry furnishings decorated the walls—jewelry, military decorations, and assorted keepsakes. The remains of a spartan meal—the bones of some roasted desert animal and a tin cup—lay beside the mat.

Yuri motioned for his "guest" to sit on one of boulders and took the other for himself.

"We have little time," Yuri told him. "Your aimless wandering allowed them to get close." It was almost a reproach.

"The samurai drugged me," Zorro replied defensively. Though it was true, the Cossack made him feel like it was a paltry excuse. Still, he received a terse nod as an acknowledgment. "Tell me about what happened at the square," asked Zorro.

Yuri exhaled in annoyance. Clearly he thought this irrelevant to their plight, but decided to indulge Zorro.

"When the rope broke, I escaped in the confusion of the attack." So Bernardo had not reached him, Zorro thought. How worried his old friend must be right now. "I found your horse, and I knew that it was yours. When you were captured, I followed." Yuri looked toward the mouth of the cave, and Zorro thought he saw the slightest smile play across his lips. "Your horse threw me twice. But in the end we agreed to rescue you together."

Revelation after revelation! So the Cossack had forged his own bond with Tornado.

"We tracked the *ronin*. You escaped. Luckily, we found you first." He looked again toward the mouth of the cave. There was not even the hint of a smile this time. "But soon, the *ronin* will find you."

"At least the odds are better with two of us—"

"I will not fight." The Cossack interrupted. His countenance discouraged debate.

"Who are you, Yuri?" Zorro cried, frustrated at the enigma that sat before him. "How can you rescue me, yet deny me help?"

"I will help," he answered simply, his gaze steady. "But I will not fight."

News that should have been encouraging had the opposite effect. Yuri, as ever, remained a contradiction. Zorro took a deep breath, willing himself to be calm.

"Then help me by explaining yourself. How you came here. I need to understand."

At first, the Cossack seemed unwilling to answer.

But Zorro would not let him look away.

"You did nothing to save yourself, yet you saved me. Now, while you still refuse to fight, you pledge your help. It is confusing."

The Russian rose suddenly, anger contorting his face further. It was a personality change Zorro had witnessed in the cantina, only this time in reverse. He tensed in case the Russian might attack.

"I am Cossack! Descended from Cossacks that fought in the Khotin War. They live off the land of Ukraine, constantly ready for battle. My great-grandfather was *hetman,* chief of his *kosh.* They wandered, they fought, savagely, against Tatars. So was I raised, surrounded by warfare and bloodshed." The Cossack had begun to pace, ensnared by the spell of his own story—one that had lacked an appreciative audience for a long time.

"In later campaigns, for the czars of Russia, I was wanderer, a murderer."

"But it was war," Zorro interjected, instantly regretting his interruption.

"But it was unnecessary!" the Cossack bellowed. "I found myself committing atrocities that make me wish for death each time I think of them. I can say nothing of the turning point, only that it came. Fleeing the army, I wandered, a true nomad like my people. But I could not escape the rage of my people's blood.

"Thinking the answer lay elsewhere, I traveled to Japan. Maybe study in the East would bring me peace. I studied with Buddhist monks—who came to fear the darkness in my soul and sent me among samurai. Other dark ones found me. I learned to kill in new ways. After much more death, I finally left Japan for this country. I want to lose myself in its vastness, find peace.

"The first night at the cantina sealed my fate. I saw the cycle starting all over again. In jail, I heard of the trap, and decided to do penance. My life for yours. Peace finally in death."

Yuri fell silent then. Zorro honored the silence. Beside them, the frail light began to sputter as the candle neared the end of its usefulness.

"You said we had little time," Zorro finally said quietly. "How will you help if you will not fight?"

The Cossack spun abruptly and plucked a fresh candle from a jumbled pile of possessions. He snapped it in half, tossing one piece back into the tangle. The remaining piece he lit with the dying flame of the original candle.

"I will train you to fight," he said. All traces of sadness and desperation had vanished. "I will teach you the *bushido*, the Way of the Warrior."

Zorro rose. "Of course. To fight the samurai, I will become a samurai."

Yuri immediately shook his head. "No. To fight samurai, to defeat *ronin*, Zorro must become greater. Truer to the nature of *kitsune*, the Japanese fox spirit. The black garments, the mask—you already look like the only warrior feared by *ronin*." His voice became a whisper:

"Ninja."

Chapter 16

"The way of the ninja is not to match strength," Yuri explained, "but to prey upon weakness." The Cossack stood before Zorro, who sat on his boulder, the student of a great master. Light from the candle seemed to burn in the foreigner's eyes.

"Ninja fight by stealth, not by confrontation." He drew himself up, almost comically, mimicking an *en garde* position, pantomiming a sword. "They do not challenge others to duels." Dropping the swordfighting stance, he stalked one of the boulders, holding an invisible dagger. "The Ninja sneaks in at night, creeps up on its prey, and slits his throat as he sleeps." Had the boulder been the Cossack's prey, its sandy blood would have stained the bed of earth surrounding it.

Zorro was aghast.

"It is not my wish to kill, unless it becomes necessary for survival." He crossed his arms, defiant.

Yuri did not argue. He just shrugged and said, "You will not kill? Then that is your weakness." He sat down on the slain boulder, quiet and impassive as he had been when Diego had first entered the jail.

Zorro knew his lesson was over. But he still needed the Cossack's help and guidance.

"Please continue," Zorro asked. "Forgive my interruption."

"You cannot become a Ninja," Yuri responded. "Ninja are assassins. You wear black, but your heart is white. Ninja have midnight in their souls." He did not rise from the boulder.

Time had truly run out if he couldn't get Yuri involved again. The packs! he suddenly thought. Perhaps their contents would revive the Cossack's interest. Zorro seized the leather bags from the ground before the candle, where Yuri had dropped them. Unbuckling the first pack quickly, Zorro poured its contents—the deadly treasures of Japan—at the Cossack's feet. *Shuriken, nunchuks,* and *kunai* rained on the floor, scattered in a semicircle around Yuri's boulder. A small wooden box struck the ground on its corner, broke open, the nameless barbs jangling as they tumbled about.

The weapons now looked as if they *had* been released from some deadly piñata. Yuri stared down at them, transfixed, a faraway gleam in his eye, and Zorro knew that the Cossack could have come from the bizarre family he had joked about with Bernardo. The Cossack's expression was exactly that of a child whose greatest birthday wish had come true.

Tenderly, Yuri reached down and plucked one of the barbed objects from the floor. In his enormous fist, the weapon looked as small as a marble. He held it out for Zorro's inspection.

"*Makibishi,*" he said.

"*Ma-ki-bi-shi,*" Zorro repeated slowly, deliberately. He then paused, allowing the exotic nature of the weapons to compel the Cossack to reveal his knowledge of them. If the man continued, then Zorro had hooked him as surely as if the barb of the *makibishi* had sunk into the Cossack's flesh.

"*Makibishi,*" Yuri said one last time. "They are scattered on ground." He pantomimed a motion similar to casting dice. "They pierce the foot of an enemy, allowing the Ninja to escape." Then with a sly grin, he added, "Maybe a good weapon for you."

Zorro returned the smile. "But I thought Ninja cut throats while their victims slept?"

The Cossack shrugged. "Sometime the victim wakes up. The ninja still does not want direct confrontation, so he tries to escape. Victim steps on spikes, ninja escapes."

"I see," Zorro nodded, still smiling although the Cossack's had faded again. "And these," he continued, lifting the second leather pack. Unfastening the buckle, he held it open for Yuri's inspection of the contents. The Cossack withdrew the chained weapons one at a time and set them side by side on the ground.

"*Kusari-gama,*" Yuri said slowly, pointing to the chain ending with a sickle. Zorro repeated the words to himself. "Cuts the enemy with a blade, or entangles and pulls away his weapon. It also wraps around the enemy, trapping his arms and legs." He then pointed to the chain ending in the metal ball. "*Manriki-gusari.* Same thing, but without the blade. It strikes the enemy with a ball instead of with a blade. The rest is the same."

"Excellent!" Zorro cried and stood abruptly. A wave of nausea struck, bringing him down on his boulder hard. As the wave receded, it carried away the hope that had been fostered by Yuri's teachings of the ways of the ninja and use of the Japanese weapons. The odds, when he finally met the Dragon Riders, would still be against him: four healthy warriors against one exhausted, drugged, and wounded masked avenger. His hope had proven to be a cork set on a beach; an ocean wave of doubt now swept it away.

Yuri seemed to perceive his thoughts.

"You still think you cannot beat them," the Cossack said, somewhat reproachfully. "Here is one from Yuri, not from the ninja. The best way to enjoy guests at a party is to invite each guest separately."

Delighted laughter burst from Zorro at the Cossack's peculiar wisdom. For Diego, social gatherings had often been more like badminton games than fiestas. The shuttlecock—Diego—would bounce from guest to guest, spending time with all but enjoying the company of none. True delight in an acquaintance, for Diego, was found during intimate lunches or suppers with a single individual. A social tactic mirrored that of a basic war tactic:

"Divide and conquer!" Zorro exclaimed. Yuri nodded affirmatively.

At that moment, the candlelight sputtered and extinguished itself. Zorro froze—the ground was still littered with a myriad of sharp objects. A few feet away, he heard a dry snap, a stone scraping, then a small flash as Yuri lit half of a new candle, nestling it in the cooling wax of the previous one. He did this all in the darkness, without injuring himself on the deadly weapons surrounding him.

"It is time," said Yuri. "They look for you."

"And what shall I do?"

"Find them first. Make *each* your prey." With the practiced neatness of Bernardo, Yuri quickly organized the jumble of weapons on the floor and began to repack the leather bags. "Take these. And remember, your sword will not save you. Only stealth and cunning.

"The way of the ninja."

"Even more," Zorro added resolutely, "the way of The Fox!"

Yuri accompanied him as they exited the cave and descended the hill to where Tornado stood waiting.

Chapter 17

Washi raged at Tanuki. "If Zorro escapes, you dishonor us all!"

The stolen horse they tracked had been located, finally. Of course, their prey was nowhere to be found. Traveling back along their path, they attempted to discover where he had dismounted.

"What honor is there in this task?" Tanuki suddenly spat back, neglecting customary deference to his leader and elder. "What honor was there ever? This Zorro is a more worthy ally than the false priest."

"We are bound!" Washi towered over the boy, but Tanuki did not back down.

"Bound, yes! Our hands and feet and souls to a madman!"

Miko sat back on her horse, alongside Baku, watching the confrontation. She agreed with both of them, knew both were entirely wrong. Confusion was coming upon her like an inexorable tide. Soon, she felt, she might drown.

Honor and duty had been ingrained in her from a young age. Yet a look in the masked man's eyes had told her that honor and duty could be found in proper action, not simply on those actions agreed-upon and promised. Where to draw the line? Certainly, Hidalgo el Cazador seemed an easy place to make those distinctions between rote honor and right honor. But was now the time, after the agreement had been made? The struggle in herself mirrored that between Washi and Tanuki. And unless they could find answers, find peace, all four of them might perish.

Baku, for his part, observed the argument from his horse, grinning lazily as ever. Occasionally, he would look down at his flute, silently fingering melodies.

"You lead us, but you follow a fiend!" Tanuki shouted, looking to his companions for support. "How dishonorably it reflects upon you, and upon the rest of us." Miko gazed at him sympathetically, unable to chose a side of the argument that would not bring about her doom. Baku's smile broadened and he nodded in a slightly mocking salutation.

"Bah! You are all weak!" Disgusted, Tanuki turned to leave.

"Tanuki!" Washi called out. Though obviously still raging, Miko thought she heard a slight conciliatory note in his voice.

"Weak?" A voice suddenly came out of the darkness. Tanuki froze. Hidalgo el Cazador materialized out of the darkness, as if emerging from the folds of his cloak. He was on foot; they had not heard his approach. The priest surveyed the group if he were as a parent preparing to punish his children. "The rest know the strength of responsibility. You were not brought to this country as an act of charity. There is a job to be done. And you will do it. You will bring me Zorro." He glared ominously at Tanuki. "Or I will kill you myself."

The priest's eyes narrowed. Miko recognized the look. Any moment now, Tanuki would fall from his horse, screaming. Sure enough, the boy did cry out. But this time, instead of falling to the ground, he launched himself at Cazador.

"No!" he cried, arms outstretched.

Cazador took one calm step backward, planted himself firmly, and raised his arms to meet Tanuki. The man may not be a samurai, Miko thought, but he was fast. Grasping the boy by the shoulders, he deftly slipped his hands into the soft joints of the *ronin*'s armor. The priest seemed impervious to the samurai's struggling and soon forced Tanuki to his knees before him. The young *ronin* groaned, his head suddenly lolling to the side like a lifeless puppet. Cazador looked down, smiled with evil satisfaction and released his grip. Tanuki slumped over on his side—dead or unconscious, Miko could not tell.

Washi jumped from his horse and knelt beside the boy. He rose in a dark rage.

"If you have harmed him . . ."

Though the *ronin* dwarfed the priest, Cazador seemed bored rather than intimidated.

"He will awaken shortly," the priest told him. "Once his blood flow returns to normal and his bone and muscles realign. And when he awakens, you will go after Zorro as you agreed."

"The boy was right—" Washi began, but the priest interrupted him.

"He was right to say that for you to lead, you must follow. It was that way in Japan with your feudal mas-

ters, and so it is with me. When you have fulfilled
your duty to me, I care not what you do. Until then,
I expect no less than your unswerving loyalty. And
his," he said, indicating Tanuki, who now groaned
and stirred. He gaze swept the rest of the group. Miko
tried to look down but not before she caught a lascivious glimmer in the priest's eyes. Even Baku's smile
faded slightly. "All of you."

With that, Hidalgo el Cazador turned his back on
them and vanished into the darkness.

The four ronin returned to the waterfall signaling
their proximity to Cazador's hidden city. Miko had
suggested the likelihood that an exhausted and con-
fused Zorro might have stopped there.

"He was here," Washi told them, examining the
disturbed earth at the bank of the pool. "And he was
not alone."

"Someone else?" Tanuki asked. "Here in the mountains?" As promised by Cazador, the boy's paralysis
had lasted only a few minutes. He now followed Washi
without question, but without enthusiasm either.

"Here is another horse." Washi pointed at the second set of hooves printed in the dirt. "Heavier than
the first. They rode up into the mountains, not back
to town."

"Could it be Cazador?" Miko wondered aloud.
"The dead city is near and he could have captured
The Fox on his own."

Washi shook his head. "I do not think so. These
tracks were made earlier than when we last saw the
priest. If he had captured Zorro, that . . . encounter . . .
would have been unnecessary." He cast a concerned
glance at Tanuki, who seemed oblivious. "This second

rider concerns me. If a bandit has chanced upon a defenseless Zorro, and he became injured or worse, matters would become quite complicated. We must find them, one way or another, and their trail is clear. That way." He pointed up into the mountains.

"We have him, then," Tanuki shrugged, without a hint of his trademark fire. They mounted their horses and began the pursuit.

The path, however clear at the start, soon disappeared in the darkness and the brush.

"We should wait until morning," Tanuki suggested. "They could be anywhere in the mountains."

"And by morning," replied Washi, "they could be anywhere else and our mission will have failed. I refuse to return to Cazador until we have succeeded."

Tanuki seemed briefly to consider the wrath of Cazador and agreed with some resignation.

Miko saw that the ordeal had all but crushed the boy's spirit and spoke up. "The four of us riding together will be easily spotted from a distance, night or day. Perhaps if we split up, we would be less obtrusive and find greater success. Zorro could have easily taken the path to Cazador's city. If so, he will have done much of our work for us."

Washi nodded after careful consideration. "You are right. But we must not venture forth alone. We'll split into pairs. You and Baku will continue along this path. Tanuki and I will return to the waterfall and follow the other route."

The matter settled, Washi and Tanuki turned back along the trail. Baku gave Miko a pleasant smile, as if they were about to share a leisurely ride in the country.

After many long minutes of riding, Miko spied a dark shape on the ground that stood out from among the patches of plants and various rocks. Horse droppings. So Zorro *had* been this way.

"Ride back and get the others," Miko told Baku.

"Washi will be displeased to discover I've left you alone, priestess," Baku replied amiably.

"He would be more displeased to find he was allowed to ride in the opposite direction of the man we must find!"

"Agreed," Baku said, nodding. "But why don't you go back? I'll make sure the droppings don't go anywhere."

Miko opened her mouth to argue, then stopped herself. While Washi was their leader, there had been no other rank assigned among them. Ordering Baku was not truly within her rights. His gentle refusal reminded her of that fact. She would go herself.

"Very well," she said conceded.

"Excellent, I will wait here."

Seeing that Baku was content to guard the trail leading to Zorro, Miko left to inform the other samurai.

From the waterfall, Washi and Tanuki followed the trail leading to the hidden city. They rode in silence at first, watching closely for any sign that Zorro had passed this way. They found none. The blue cast of the moon was fading as it dropped lower in the sky. Dawn would break soon. Washi hoped the ordeal would be over by then.

"Isn't this country fascinating?" he asked suddenly. He wanted to find something that would stop the boy's brooding. "It is so much different than our own."

"But the same, in some respects," Tanuki finally sighed. "We are outlaws here, as well."

"It is only the circumstance, boy," Washi told him. "We'll be free of Cazador soon enough."

The boy frowned, unconvinced. "As long as I have nightmares I will never be free of him."

Unexpectedly, the samurai leader gave him a fatherly pat on the back. "You underestimate your strength, Tanuki." He pointed east, inviting the soldier to look beyond the mountains ahead in his mind's eye. "This land, from what I hear, is wide, the size of several Japans laid end to end. And nearly as tall. There are entire mountain ranges to place between ourselves and Cazador. And we will."

"When it's over?" Tanuki asked.

"When it's over." Washi stated this definitively. Cazador had battered the mind and spirit of his young charge. He needed assurances that everything would be all right. And though his resolve had repeatedly faltered in Cazador's presence, Washi was ultimately certain that everything would indeed work out for the best.

They had ridden quite a distance from the waterfall—the others would be twice that in the other direction. Soon, Washi and Tanuki would turn back because the trail had gone cold.

"Wait!" the younger *ronin* suddenly cried, leaping from his horse. A dark smudge lay on the ground before them.

"What is it?" asked the older samurai.

"Horse droppings. Fresh. The Fox has been this way. And recently."

"So, the trail leading in the other direction was false," Washi realized aloud. Leave it to a fox to lead a merry chase. "Hurry back to Miko and Baku. Bring them here. If Zorro is not alone, we may need the others."

"What will you do?"

"Locate Zorro and follow at a discreet distance. We'll attack as a group when you bring the others. Perhaps he'll save us all the effort and simply surrender."

"I would prefer that he did at this point," Tanuki said.

"Go, and return with Miko and Baku. Let's share in the final capture of The Fox together."

He clapped Tanuki on the back, sending him racing toward the other *ronin*. The Fox was within their grasp once more.

Chapter 18

Zorro watched the samurai from a bluff high above the trail. He noted that although they were clad in armor, they had not worn their helmets. The group stopped suddenly, and after a few minutes' debate, two of the *ronin* turned back toward the waterfall.

Perfect, he thought. As he expected, their need to find him was urgent enough to divide the group. Still, the odds were not to Zorro's liking. Virtually unarmed, slowed by the waning effects of the drugs and the pain of his injuries, any two of them could subdue or kill him easily. If the Cossack had only joined him. . . . But Yuri was adamant in his refusal to fight. He did, however, fulfill his promise to help. For that reason, Zorro had sent him along the second path leading from the waterfall. If he guessed properly, Zorro figured the Cossack would have placed the horse droppings in the path by now.

Familiar with tracking, he knew that horse droppings were signs of passage as indelible as tracks. His plan had been to deposit the droppings in the second path, leading the two groups farther apart. Yuri had approved of the plan and readily agreed to help by planting the false evidence of their passage.

On foot, Zorro stalked the remaining riders, Miko and Baku. Sure enough, they happened upon Tornado's droppings. Which would go to bring the others? he wondered as he watched. The moment one left, the clock would begin ticking. He would strike at the remaining samurai, waiting long enough that the departing *ronin* would not hear the struggle and return.

When Miko turned back along the trail, Zorro was almost relieved. He did not relish their inevitable clash. The smiling samurai, however, was another story.

Using the sound of Miko's horse to cover his movements, Zorro descended the bluff. Patches of the aptly named brittle bush dotted his path, ready to snap at the slightest misstep. His black clothing helped conceal him in the near darkness, but he was now willing himself into total invisibility.

He crept closer.

Baku sat on his horse, lifting his flute to his lips, appearing to play melodies, but making no noise.

A twig broke under Zorro's foot and Baku looked in his direction, instantly alert. Zorro froze. He would not move, not even breathe. He thought of himself not as a bush, but the space between its branches, the shadows on a rock at night. Baku soon relaxed and resumed his silent flute-playing.

He managed to find himself within a dozen yards of the samurai. Slipping his hand from his pocket, he withdrew a *shuriken*. Deadly as it could be, Zorro hoped that it would only provide an annoyance.

Uncoiling the chain of the *manriki-gusari* as quietly as possible, Zorro laid it on the ground next to him. He then withdrew a single throwing star and sighted the *ronin*'s horse.

If he could slice a rope at a hundred feet with a dagger, surely he could strike a nearby horse with a throwing star. For the sake of discipline, he drew the mental line anyway—from his hand to the horse— and snapped his wrist, flinging the *shuriken* away.

Several points of the throwing star pierced the inner thigh of the rear leg farthest from Zorro. Mostly likely, it felt like a snake bite. Sure enough, the previously motionless horse started to stamp in place. Whinnying, it shook its leg, attempting to dislodge the *shuriken*. Baku lowered his flute and attempted to calm his mount with soothing words.

That had been the easy part—now came the difficult task. Taking one end of the chain in his left hand, he tossed the metal ball with his right. The ball flew past the horse's forelegs, the samurai too busy trying to calm his horse to notice. With sharp tug, the ball reversed direction, causing the chain to wrap around the agitated horse's forelegs. Still in pain, it reared, both hooves leaving the ground. Zorro gave one light tug to make sure the chain had wrapped tightly around its target. It had.

Grasping the chain with both hands Zorro raised himself and pulled with all of his might. Baku saw him then, but the surprise froze him in place. He could not conceive of how Zorro had appeared, or what he was doing. Snared by the chain, the horse's legs were twisted out from under its body. Bucking as it fell over on its side, it threw the samurai screaming into a tangle of scrub oak. There was a loud crack as he landed. Unable to see through the great cloud of dust displaced by the falling horse, Zorro dashed forward, holding the small wooden box.

From beyond the cloud, the *ronin* continued wailing, his screams mingling with the horse's in a chorus of mortal agony. He had to silence them both before their cries summoned the others.

Emerging from the cloud, he opened the wooden box and shook it. The small barbs of the *makibishi* scattered over the desert floor between him and the *ronin*. Finally, he could see as well as hear the other man, whose back was to Zorro, kneeling as if prayer. Had Zorro wished to do so, he could sneak up behind the vulnerable *ronin* and slit his throat before he could react.

The way of the ninja, perhaps, he thought. But not the way of Zorro.

The horse continued to scream in pain, but the *ronin*'s cries had become sobs. Zorro drew the *katana* he had stolen from Tanuki earlier, the sound of the blade scraping against the leather scabbard meant for his own sword catching the *ronin*'s attention. His head straightened as if listening. Then with amazing quickness he rose and spun. However, instead of his sword, he presented another object, held out tenderly in both hands as if it were a child.

His flute, shattered in two. Resting on the desert floor behind the *ronin*, Zorro could see a large stone on which the flute had landed. Tears gave way to rage. With one hand, the *ronin* gripped the collar of his armor, manipulated a catch with thumb and tore the breastplate from his chest, throwing it away into the desert. The back half fell and landed like an upended turtle behind him. Casting the broken flute to one side, the *ronin* drew his *katana*.

Zorro raised his, prepared for battle. With an enraged growl, the *ronin* stomped forward to the attack—the growl ascending into a scream again as pain racked his left foot. He had stepped on a *makibishi*, hiding like a scorpion in the dust, driving one barb up into his foot. Hopping onto his right foot, he stepped on yet another barb, sending him spinning around in agony and falling backwards toward Zorro, who had to jump back to avoid losing both his feet to the *ronin*'s razor-sharp blade.

The musician's cry was suddenly choked off. He writhed on the ground madly, arms clawing his back. As Zorro approached, he saw another barb hooked into the flesh of the *ronin*'s left arm. A trickle of blood ran from the corner of his mouth, coagulating in the dust that covered the man's face.

Zorro stood over him, and incredibly, when their eyes met again, the ronin managed a smile. He said something in Japanese that Zorro could not understand. When the *ronin* repeated the same sounds and saw that his opponent couldn't grasp his meaning, he turned onto one side, with great effort, coughing blood but continuing to smile. Seeing his back, Zorro understood what the man had been saying, what he was now showing him. The *ronin* had fallen upon several *makibishi* barbs, which protruded from the his back. At least two had been driven deep enough to puncture his lungs. The man was going to die.

The *ronin* rolled onto his back again, wincing as the barbs were driven deeper into him. A fresh flow of blood rushed over his lips. Still, he smiled. A ripple of calm spread over the *ronin*.

The musician's right hand went to his sword, which

lay just within his reach. Zorro raised his *katana* slightly in defense, but knew he was in no danger. The injured man simply smiled more brightly, and uttered more words in Japanese. Remembering that Zorro did not understand him, he showed his meaning by stretching his right hand out, toward the *shakuhachi*. His fingers clawed the earth uselessly. Only this dimmed the smile on his face. Then he seemed to be pleading in Japanese.

Zorro turned to retrieve the flute. Hopefully, it would comfort the *ronin*. He would bring help if he could, but knew that even under the best of circumstances, the man only had a few hours to live. Perhaps if he could convince the others to suspend their deadly mission in order to save their friend . . . but he couldn't count on that.

As he lifted the flute, Zorro heard the musician cough with effort. Turning, he found the *ronin* had raised his sword, grasping the hilt with both hands. The point of blade rested against his own abdomen.

"No!" Zorro cried and reached forward.

But it was too late. With a quick, efficient motion, the *ronin* pierced his body, then wrested the blade upward. More blood rushed over the samurai's lips, which still managed to hold a pleasant smile despite the mortal wound. Taking one hand from his sword, grinning through the pain, the *ronin* reached again for his beloved instrument. As if in a dream, Zorro saw himself handing the flute to the *ronin*, who nodded his head appreciatively. Clutching the *shakuhachi* beside him like a lover, the *ronin* returned both hands to the hilt of his sword. With one final tug, he drew the blade up into his chest, cleaving his heart. Coughing and sputtering, he died a moment later, but his amiable smile lived on.

Zorro closed the samurai's vacant eyes, then retrieved the flute he had been trying to reach. Laying the pieces across the *ronin*'s body, Zorro turned sadly and whistled. Tornado appeared from not far up the path. He mounted the stallion and set off after the woman.

Miko had nearly arrived at the waterfall when she heard a horse approaching from behind at a hard gallop. Reining her horse, they turned around to face the oncoming rider. Instinctively, her hand fell to the hilt of her *katana*.

Hopefully, it was only Baku with something to report. But now that she was on her own, it would do to remain alert.

The horse came into view in the dim light. Not Baku's horse. A larger, heavier steed. She drew her sword.

As it neared, she could see that it was riderless. Packs hung at its sides, an empty saddle clung to its back. She spurred her horse toward the stallion. Perhaps Baku had clashed with Zorro and had unhorsed him, frightening the stallion away.

Looking into the horse's eyes, she knew the last was probably untrue. Its fierce gaze said that he feared nothing.

But if Zorro and Baku were engaged in battle, she should return to help. Replacing the sword into its scabbard, she started back, ignoring the stallion that now passed very close.

So intent on returning to Baku, she did not see the dark shape hanging beneath the large horse. A hand reached out, grasped her ankle and she was dragged from her saddle. Dust rose in a cloud around her as she landed on her back. Though stunned, she never lost sight of the great horse, which reared before her. The shape underneath detached itself, using the momentum of the stallion's movement to fly upward.

When all four hooves hit the ground again, Zorro sat astride the horse. He smiled devilishly.

For a moment, she was paralyzed. The beating of his heart returned to her, the warmth of his skin. She shook away the memories that clouded her mind and sapped her will. He would no doubt kill her as easily as he had unhorsed her given the chance. Returning to herself, Miko rolled to her feet and drew her *katana* with one smooth motion. In her mind, she now viewed her feelings back at the camp with disgust. Baku was right to make lewd insinuations. Her weakness had been exposed. Her vacillations between right and wrong, duty and honor, all weakness.

The Fox's smile had exposed these flaws, the light in his eyes. The heartbeat had echoed them. First the spell of the false priest, now the spirit of the *kitsune* tainted her. She would exorcise both demons. Zorro's heart would beat its last at the end of her blade.

She leapt at the man on the horse.

Instead of dodging the *ronin*'s attack, Zorro welcomed it. He ducked to the side, grabbed her wrists and threw himself backwards. Pulling her over Tornado's back, they both landed in the dirt. He must be careful—he had not been able to hold a sword while he hung from Tornado's underside, and her quick recovery had not allowed him to draw one.

The woman landed on top of Zorro, their faces only inches apart. Their eyes locked and their struggling ceased. He nearly kissed her; and he thought she would have accepted it. Instead, she smashed her forehead into his. Stars now exploded in his head with the blow.

She rolled from his grasp prepared to attack. Murder gleamed in her eyes, as if he had actually stolen an offensive kiss. The *ronin* cried out in Japanese and brought down her sword.

"No more enchantment!" Miko cried. She had felt the powerful draw of *kitsune*'s eyes when they had fallen together. This one was much less powerful than Cazador, yet more insidious. The lure of pleasure and contentment was more enticing than the priest's crude visions, yet would surely lead to her ruin all the same.

The swordsman lay on the ground, unarmed. It would normally be dishonorable to strike a harmless opponent, but her fury overtook her. She had to end the torture of her mind being prodded and poked.

Miko's sword struck a rock as she realized that, in her fury, her eyes had been closed. The shock traveled up her arms and nearly caused her to drop the *katana*. Zorro had avoided her blow, rolling onto his stomach. Springing from his arms, he launched himself from the ground, both feet striking her armored torso. Arms pinwheeling, she finally let go of her sword. Zorro quickly kicked it from her reach and turned to his horse. Without her sword, he knew she was no less dangerous—she could disable him with a blow, and appeared ready to do so.

Miko bounded at Zorro just as he turned back to face her. She realized too late that he was swinging something rapidly. She saw the flash of a blade attached to a thin chain. Zorro stepped back as the blade completed one orbit around her, the chain beginning to pull tight across her upper arms. Quickly, he helped the blade along and was suddenly behind her, pulling the chain tight, trapping her. That didn't make her helpless, however. She kicked back with one leg, but he had expected the move. Avoiding the blow,

Zorro swept both legs out from under her, and she fell to the ground. By the time she had recovered, he had wrapped a similar chain, this one ending in a metal ball, around her legs. She was immobilized.

Instead of ensnaring her soul, the *kitsune* had trapped her body.

The Fox stood above her, the devilish smile returning to his face. He was speaking, but she couldn't understand. More enchantment, she thought. Or perhaps, words of condemnation.

"You don't mind waiting there while I retrieve your companions, do you?" Of course, she did not answer. Only terror gleamed in her eyes. Clearly, she thought he meant to kill her.

"No, I won't do that," he said, trying to soften his tone to convey meaning. Her expression relaxed a bit, but only to wary confusion. "And I won't let you kill yourself, either." He had retrieved her *katana*. Presenting it to her made her squirm—her fears had been reignited.

"No no!" he said quickly and hid it from sight.

"Zorro!" came a resonant voice. Yuri, riding a burro, appeared on the path from the waterfall. "The young one. He returns."

"Then I'd best go," Zorro replied, leaping into Tornado's saddle. "Will you watch this one until I return?"

Yuri frowned. "What of the other *ronin*?" His eyes never left the female samurai. She looked up, fear and confusion melting into another, unfathomable expression.

"Dead, I'm afraid," said Zorro, shaking his head. "Killed himself. I couldn't stop him."

"You cannot stop *seppuku*," the Cossack replied.

"Ritual suicide is part of the samurai code. Better to kill oneself rather than to be captured in battle or dishonored by failure."

"That's a rather bleak way of looking at things," Zorro told him.

"It is the samurai code," Yuri repeated. Zorro said nothing; this was a man who himself would rather die than fight. That was *his* code.

"I'll go after the others," Zorro stated. The Cossack said nothing.

Washi arrived at the boulder marking the entrance to the hidden city. He had seen no other signs that Zorro had ridden this way. Certainly, he had not entered the city. They had lost him.

How could this be? Tanuki himself said the droppings were fresh. Perhaps Cazador's manipulations had clouded his judgment. Or worse, they had fallen prey to a crude but effective deception.

In either case, his party had been divided, then divided again. Tanuki traveled alone. What of Miko and Baku? The *ronin* leader wheeled his horse around and spurred him to race back to the waterfall. They must regroup. The countryside seemed foreboding now, not vast and romantic as the fantasies he'd foolishly allowed himself.

He leaned forward on his mount, whipping it with the reins.

Zorro arrived on horseback at the waterfall just as the youngest *ronin* was rounding the pool. The boy saw him and charged forward on his steed without hesitation. There would be no tricks with this one, Zorro realized. Drawing Miko's katana, he prepared for battle.

Like jousting medieval knights, the two clashed on the banks before the pool. The boy was quick and used his free arm to strike at Zorro. Both were knocked to the ground. Instinctively, they released each other and rolled away from the horses.

Zorro rose to his feet to face the samurai. The boy now held two blades: in one hand, a *katana* similar to the blades the others used, and in the other, a smaller version, what Yuri had described as a *kogatana*. Zorro only had one blade. It would have to do.

The *ronin* attacked with the longer blade. This was easily parried, but the boy brought the *kogatana* across his chest, nearly disemboweling him, Zorro barely twisted away in time. The blades whirled again as the *ronin* pressed his attack. Zorro was driven back, blocking one strike after another, each a hairsbreadth closer to causing him injury—or death—than the last. His opponent had become a relentless machine, arms spinning, blades a dull blur as they sought his flesh.

The intensity of the attack was taking its toll on Zorro. The other fights had been over quickly enough for him not to notice his lingering infirmities. Under the pressure of battle, they reasserted themselves.

Another jab with the *katana*, but this time a feint, and the *kogatana* raked his rib, reopening his earlier wound. The boy was winning. And he knew it.

That strike had drawn blood! It would not be long now.

The sight of Zorro had been unexpected, but welcome. Tanuki gave little thought to his comrades as he charged, for now would be the time of his release. He would strike down Zorro, deliver his body to Cazador personally, then they would be free. He would never have to face the dragon again.

As admirably as The Fox was fighting, it was clear that he was wearing down. Soon, he would have to collapse from exhaustion, in defeat, or—so be it!—death.

But no tricks this time. Tanuki would not be taken for a fool again.

Tanuki drove the masked man to the edge of the lake. Soon, he would land a second blow. Then a third. A fourth would surely mean his death. The *ronin* was coming to welcome that moment.

Just then, Zorro found a hidden reserve of strength. In a furious attack of his own, he drove Tanuki back. Several blows would actually have caused injury, had the samurai not been wearing his armor. As it was, Zorro only managed to put some space between the two of them. His chest was heaving. Clearly his flurry had been an effort of last resort. Tanuki would end the battle now.

Then the man did a most curious thing: he whistled.

As expected, his odd gesture caused the boy to pause. The sudden galloping noise—Tornado answering his summons—further disoriented the *ronin,* allowing Zorro to strike the *katana* from the boy's hand. A sweeping kick knocked the *kogatana* from the boy's other hand; it went spinning end over end into the lake.

Zorro had effectively turned the tables. Though disarmed, however, the boy still had fight in him. The *ronin* actually growled and seemed ready to match his fists against Zorro's blade. Furious, he charged. Zorro evened the odds and cast away his sword. The two grappled before the waterfall.

The *ronin* landed a lightning series of punches to

Zorro's head, staggering him. Blood flowed from a split lip.

He became aware that a horse was approaching; not Tornado, who had only gone a few steps.

Zorro blocked another round of punches and landed one of his own. Doing so was worse for him than for the boy—his fist nearly shattered against the lacquered wooden armor. His pain made the boy laugh.

The approaching horse was closer. Clearly, the sound came from the northern path. The boy heard it too and smiled. No doubt the *ronin* leader was coming.

Soon it would be two against one. Even if he managed to defeat the young *ronin*, he would have no energy left to confront the older one. The battle would be over finally. The youth needed only to wait for his ally to seal Zorro's fate.

Instead, the boy apparently wanted Zorro as a trophy. He abruptly launched into a flying kick clearly meant to finish Zorro off. But the boy had misjudged, giving Zorro plenty of time and distance in which to react. Stepping to the side, he seized the boy's leg in both hands and pulled it past him. As the *ronin*'s body sailed past, he quickly smashed his elbow into the boy's back, adding to his momentum and sending the *ronin* flying into the pool several yards from the water's edge. The boy started thrashing immediately.

The *ronin* leader emerged from the north trail a moment later.

Zorro turned to face the final *ronin* and considered his options. By the looks of things, fighting the leader would result in two deaths. The most immediate was his: he was unarmed once more and exhausted. The rage on the *ronin*'s face indicated he would spare

Zorro no quarter. But the *ronin* could not kill him fast enough to save the boy, whose armor was now filling with water. Soon, he would sink into the pool and drown.

The *ronin*'s horse was only a few paces away. In seconds, the blade would come down, ending two lives.

Zorro dove into the pool. The blade missed him by inches.

Kicking hard, he propelled himself to the figure whose struggles were weakening. Throwing one arm around the *ronin*'s neck, he lifted the boy's head above the water. While the boy didn't fight him, the effort almost caused Zorro to go under. With the last of his strength, he dragged the boy toward the edge of the pool. The distance felt like miles. Before he could reach the edge, his strength gave out entirely. The *ronin* became an anvil on his chest. Unable to pull free, the boy's armor would drag them both down. Zorro closed his eyes.

Chapter 19

"**Y**our hand," came a harsh voice. Through the haze, Zorro recognized it as the *ronin* leader's. "Give me your hand."

Dragging himself back to consciousness, he looked toward the shore. The *ronin* leader was there, reaching for them. Adjusting his hold on the boy, he stretched his arm back. The older *ronin* leaned farther out. Their hands clasped. Zorro and the boy were hauled toward the edge of the pool.

As he helped the boy onto the shore, Zorro's head went under twice. Each time, the older *ronin* grabbed him by the collar and pulled him up once more. Then the Dragon Rider hoisted him bodily onto the bank. He lay on his back beside the boy. Water rushed in gouts from the joints in the *ronin*'s armor.

"You speak Spanish?" Zorro managed weakly. The lead Dragon Rider crouched beside him.

"*Sí,*" he answered. His voice was low and gruff, but not unpleasant. A trace of sadness tinged his voice. He was remembering days past, never to be recovered. He placed a hand over his heart. "I am Washi. That is Ta-nuki."

"Zorro," he replied as he sat up. The *ronin* nodded. "This is what an educated man finds himself doing?" Zorro asked.

"I could asked the same of you." He spoke not un-kindly. "What of the others?"

"The woman is up the trail. She is being guarded." The *ronin* nodded. "And Baku?"

Zorro assumed it was the musician's name. He shook his head. "Dead, I'm afraid. Killed himself. *Seppuku.*"

Another nod, but with no surprise or sadness. "*Sep-puku,*" he repeated.

The boy suddenly coughed and raised himself up on his elbows. At the sight of Zorro beside him, he began to scramble away. The older *ronin* put a hand on his shoulder to calm him and said something in Japanese. The boy became wide-eyed.

"He does not believe you saved his life." The man frowned. "Even I don't understand. We were sent to capture you. We are the instruments of your death."

"Will you kill me now?"

The *ronin* frowned again and turned back to the boy. They exchanged words in Japanese, frequently looking at Zorro. It became a heated debate.

"It is a problem," he sighed told Zorro finally. "We are honor-bound to deliver you to one called Cazador."

"Ah!" So the Aztec had escaped the gold cave after all. "We are . . . acquainted."

"We have a duty to him to bring you. Yet your ac-tions place us in your debt as well."

"Were you meant to be my executioners?" Zorro saw a glimmer of hope.

"No. Cazador reserved that right."

"Then take me." Zorro replied. "I go willingly. You will have discharged your duties, and I can deal with Cazador myself." He stood, and the world began spinning. After a few deep breaths, the dizzy spell passed. "In the morning, that is. I suggest we camp first and rest up."

Washi explained Zorro's idea to Tanuki. He seemed to argue at first, but the older *ronin* insisted. Turning to Zorro, he sounded apologetic.

"The boy is terrified of Cazador. The priest makes him relive terrible experiences." He spoke with fatherly concern.

"I understand," Zorro replied truthfully. "I, too, have looked into his eyes." He spoke these words directly to Tanuki. Despite the language barrier, the boy seemed to comprehend. "Let's find the others, rest for a while, and you can take me to where Cazador is hiding."

"Agreed," said Washi.

The three rose, collected their weapons and mounted their horses. Taking the east trail, they headed to where Zorro had left Yuri and Miko.

Only Yuri remained. He sat in the same position as Zorro had left him, staring at the chains, which lay coiled on the ground like dead snakes. The sickle was missing from the *kusari-gama*. The Cossack looked up at the trio, registering no surprise. Zorro jumped down from Tornado's saddle.

"Where is the woman?" Zorro asked. One link of the kusari-gama chain had been pried open against a rock.

"She escaped."

Zorro looked at Yuri in exasperation, then to the *ronin*. "Would she have gone to Cazador?"

"No doubt," Washi answered. "But he will be very displeased if she returns bringing news of failure." He quickly translated the conversation into Japanese for Tanuki. The boy replied excitedly, and appeared ready to ride away from them.

"He is worried for her," Washi explained. "As am I. I would not have any of us face him alone. We cannot wait to rest."

"I thought not. Let's go." Despite his exhaustion, Zorro's smile was as brilliant as ever.

Branches clawed at her face and threatened to knock her from her horse. Miko raced at breakneck speed back to Cazador's hidden city. Even so, her stallion barely kept pace with the torrent of thoughts running through her mind. . . .

The man with whom Zorro had left her had made no move to harm her; he simply watched. His eyes were quite different than The Fox's or Cazador's. They contained all the power, yet none of the force. No images of pleasure or pain were conjured by them. They were neither comforting nor threatening. Nevertheless, she found herself surprisingly lost in them, not because he had drawn her out, but because she had entered them willingly.

The guard registered no emotion, but continued to stare, aware of her scrutiny. Oddly, she felt no embarrassment, as she had with Zorro. The steady gaze gave her no discomfort. It was like being bathed in a radiant amber light, rather than the garish intensity of Cazador's will or scorched by the passion of Zorro. And somehow, lying bound in the mountains of a country not her own, watched over by a strange man, a strange calm had settled over her. Her awareness sharpened. And she realized that in his haste, Zorro had neglected to remove the sickle-shaped blade atop the *kusari-gama* he had used to ensnare her.

Twisting her body so her back—and the sickle—were out of the man's sight she began to speak to him. Miko did not expect the man to understand, but it would be enough to distract him while she attempted to wedged the tip of the blade through one link of the thin chain.

"Won't you help me?" she asked in Japanese.

"I cannot help," the man replied perfectly in Japanese. Her surprise stilled the hand with which she now grasped the sickle. "I need not. Zorro will not kill you."

She found no comfort in his words despite the honesty in his voice. And the continuous glow in his eyes. He had not *yet* killed her, of course, but this battle was meant to end in the death of Zorro. And if not his death, then hers and the rest of the *ronin*. It was the Way of the Warrior.

Miko resumed the task of freeing herself. The dagger's blade was extremely sharp and strong, sturdier than the chain to which it was attached. And if she could position it properly against the rock she felt against her back, she could open the link and remove the chain trapping her arms. Still, she was only yards from the man. He could stop her easily. The blade twisted the wrong way and nicked her wrist. Miko cried out.

The man's expression didn't change. He just continued to watch.

"I will not alter your fate," he said suddenly.

He knew, of course. But he would not stop her escape. Testing the theory, she applied greater pressure to the link. If she were wrong, or the man lying, he would take the blade from her and indeed they would have to wait to see what Zorro would serve up as her fate. If not . . .

A clash of metal rang in the distance. More fighting.

The guard glanced in that direction for a moment, then back down at her.

The link popped open. In a few moments, she had shrugged free of the *kusari-gama*. Unwrapping her legs from the *manriki-gusari*, she pulled the sickle from its chain and brandished it at the stranger. Perhaps he just wanted an excuse to fight, to kill her. He did not stand. He simply regarded her with the same even gaze. Even when she brought the sickle to his throat.

"I could kill you," she growled. Some of her anger at being captured was bubbling to the surface.

"Yes," he said quietly, looking up at her steadily. He did not plead for his life. Nor did he seem anxious to die. He would not even alter his own fate. It was up to her.

Miko withdrew the blade and mounted her horse, which had been tethered nearby. She heard no more sounds of battle coming from the direction of the waterfall. If the others prevailed against Zorro, they would return to gather her and Baku before bringing their quarry to Cazador. If Zorro had beaten them somehow, he would come for her. She did not want to face him alone.

One way or another, she would need to find Baku. With a final glance at her mysterious guard, Miko turned and rode up the eastern trail, away from the waterfall.

Out of the amber light of the stranger's gaze, Miko's serenity faltered. It fled entirely at the sight of Baku's corpse lying beside that of his fallen horse. So, Zorro *did* kill. With that came the conviction that Washi and Tanuki had been slain by the *kitsune*. Miko panicked. Spurring her horse, she rode a new trail back to the hidden city. Miko did not want to pass the fallen bodies of any more of her comrades. Loath as she was to go to him, Cazador was all she had left.

The sun had just begun to peer over the horizon when Miko arrived at the entrance to the city. She rode her horse past the rock and dismounted. Her feet barely touched the ground and she took off running, leaving her bow and other supplies behind. The streets were a maze of pillars and buildings all marked with the form of a jaguar. Finally, she reached the entrance of Cazador's half-completed temple. Taking the sloping passageway, she found him below, standing before the raised altar, like a real priest awaiting the arrival of his flock.

He smiled. And her skin crawled.

"Miko, my dear," he said in Japanese. "Where are your companions?"

"They are . . . Baku is dead." Her mind was a jumble once more in this evil man's presence.

"Terrible." Cazador seemed utterly unmoved. "And the others?"

She could only gape silently. Only then did his shark's smile darken.

"Most importantly, where is Zorro?" His voice increased in volume and menace. She could only stare dumbly. Then the veneer of the smile returned. "Come here, my dear Miko. No need for us to be shouting our conversation across the room." He held out his hand as if he were asking her to dance.

She unwillingly moved toward him. Her body inhabited another world; sand scraped beneath her feet.

"So, Zorro has proven to be a match for the Dragon Riders after all." He continued to hold out his hand. She continued to move toward him. "Four of you." He shook his head like a disappointed parent. "Amazing."

Miko now stood before the stone alter. Cazador gestured down at the cold, stone surface of the altar. She followed with her eyes, as if they were attached to them by a string.

"I've shown you this, of course." He did not wait for her to answer. "A sacrificial altar to the Aztec gods. A virgin would lay upon it, then the priest would take this," abruptly he held up a dagger—Miko jumped but could not tear her eyes away—"and cut out the girl's still-beating heart in offering."

He let the image hang between them for a moment, then added, "She was conscious and offered herself willingly."

Cazador led her eyes with the dagger until he held it before his face. Lowering the blade, her eyes remained fixed by his. He was casting a spell again. The urge to resist passed quickly through her mind and was gone. Her mind had been ensnared the moment she had entered the temple.

"Look down, Miko," he commanded solemnly. "Below the altar. See them?"

Obeying silently, she looked to the ground. About a foot from the base of the altar, the stone began to slope down. At the lowest point, at the center, was a metal grate. Each side sported a similar grate.

With the point of the dagger, Cazador traced an imaginary path down the side of the altar to a grate.

"The blood of the sacrificed girl would flow down, then through the gutters and be washed away. The priests would have the top of the alter cleaned between sacrifices, but not the sides. It became a work of art of sorts. Every sacrifice would cause a different pattern of blood to flow down. The effect was much like the base of a candlestick that has held candles of many different colors of wax." He uttered a reptilian laugh. "Of course, this work was painted in one color. Different shades."

Miko was mortified by his words. She wished to flee

but found no muscle would obey her mind's commands to turn and run.

"I meant Zorro to be the first sacrifice on this altar. Of course, he's not exactly what the gods want; but then, this one is for me, not for them. Besides, Zorro's blood would be as good as any to test the workings of the drainage system, don't you think?"

Miko nodded dully.

"Then again, your blood will work as well. And perhaps please the gods at the same time. What do you think of that?"

Again, Miko nodded.

"Take off your breastplate, Miko," he said evenly. "It will be difficult enough to cut through your bones."

Nodding again like a zombie, Miko removed the upper portion of her armor. The cloth tunic beneath was soaked with sweat from the day's exertions.

"Make yourself comfortable." With a sweeping gesture, Cazador indicated the altar. Against her will, Miko found herself climbing onto the altar and lying on her back. Out of the corner of her eye, the dagger glinted in the torch light.

"No." She said, her voice barely audible.

"Yes," Cazador replied, his voice gentle as a lover's. Then he raised the dagger.

Chapter 20

Washi led the group to the hidden city. Dawn arrived minutes before they stopped before a large boulder.

"Here," said Washi. He dismounted and the rest followed suit.

Zorro turned to Yuri, who had ridden with him on Tornado. The Cossack was the only one not holding a weapon.

"You have come this far. Join us. Take up a weapon against Cazador, if only for show."

"If I pick up weapon, I will use it," Yuri replied. "And I do not wish to kill."

"Watch the horses, then," Zorro told him sternly. "I can understand your desire to avoid violence, but not your willingness to let people die needlessly. If this woman dies, it will be on your head for letting her go."

The Cossack did not reply, which was just as well. Time grew short and Zorro would brook no argument.

"Let us hurry," Zorro said, turning to the others.

"This way." Washi let them past the boulder and into the hidden city. Zorro stopped in amazement at what lay before him. Cazador had enthralled many more people than anyone had guessed to have accomplished this feat along with the pyramid at Rayos del Sol. Still, the city's emptiness and the half-completed condition of most of the structures made the compound seem more like a cemetery than a seat of power.

"He will be there," Washi told him, pointing at the incomplete pyramid standing against a far rock wall. "Hurry," Washi said, and they wended their way through the ruins.

Inside the entrance to the pyramid, Washi began walking toward what appeared to be a throne room. After a few steps, however, they all heard it: a voice coming from below. Hidalgo el Cazador. The priest's voice floated up from a passageway to the right of the pyramid's entrance.

With as much stealth as possible, the group hurried down the passage to the bowels of the pyramid. It opened into a large room, dominated by a stone altar. Against the back wall, two jaguar statues stood guard in a room that was otherwise featureless. Miko lay prone on the slab. Behind her, Hidalgo el Cazador stood, a dagger raised, ready to plunge it into her chest. He seemed delighted by the intrusion.

"So! You have prevailed against Zorro after all!" He lowered the dagger slightly. Then he frowned, noticing that Zorro was not a prisoner. "So you have made a bargain, have you? Your *bushido* code of honor is much more flexible than I would have thought."

"You have never been honorable," Washi shouted at him. They took a step into the room. Cazador raised the dagger once more.

"Perhaps, but I will give you a chance to regain your honor in my eyes. Seize Zorro now. Hand him to me. I will return your precious Miko. With her heart still intact."

"No!" Washi cried without hesitation. "Let her go and face us."

Cazador laughed. "Four against one? I doubt I would fare as well as Zorro against those odds. And since I do not plan on surrendering, I might as well whittle the odds more to my favor."

Cazador turned his attention back to Miko and his body tensed. He would bring the dagger down on Miko, and they were too far to do anything about it.

Just then, there came a shout from behind them. Zorro recognized the meaning, even if he didn't understand the actual words, and threw himself to the side, as did the samurai—as they had in the square.

A thin blur raced past them and suddenly, Cazador flew backwards, dropping the dagger with a shout of pain. Zorro and the samurai turned.

Yuri stood in the passageway, still holding Miko's bow.

"I could not let the woman die," the Cossack said quietly. "I must no longer be a murderer, must stop embracing death; and I must, for once, fight for life."

"Good man," Zorro told him. They all hurried to Miko. Against the back wall of the altar room, Cazador lay clutching his dagger hand, which had been pierced by an arrow. The Aztec crawled quickly along the wall until he was between the two jaguar statuettes, where Zorro confronted him. Cazador sat up, flattening his back against the wall.

"Run me through, will you, Zorro?" Cazador challenged him, his voice laced with pain. "I suppose you think you deserve the pleasure."

"It would be no pleasure, so I will refrain," Zorro replied. "I wish only to see you in a room more befitting your true station in life: a jail cell."

Behind him, Miko moaned as she started to recover from Cazador's trance. Zorro glanced back—Yuri's usual apathy had vanished. The Cossack seemed to be taking quite an interest in her well-being.

Cazador, meanwhile, saw his chance and took it.

He struck out with the hand from which the arrow still protruded. The point sank into Zorro's leg, and with a scream, Cazador tore his hand free from the arrow. Zorro clutched at his wound and retreated.

Still seated, Cazador kicked the jaguar statue to his right. Instead of falling or shattering, it simply pivoted on its base, leaning to the right. There came a click, then a deep rumble emanated from the ceiling. Dust and sand shook loose from above. A scraping sound was heard and sand began to fall more heavily. The debris was not coming from the stones themselves but falling through holes that began to appear in the ceiling.

As the rain of sand increased, dust rose, blinding the group. Grit sought their eyes and lungs. Zorro raised an arm to shield his face. His last image of Cazador was of the false priest kicking at the jaguar statue to his left. Then, the fall of sand became torrential, threatening to smother them all. A hand grasped his shoulder.

"Come!" shouted Washi above the roar of the falling sand. He yanked Zorro, hobbling on his injured leg, toward the passageway leading out of the pyramid. The others struggled ahead of them on treacherous dunes that had formed on the floor. Yuri helped Miko, a great bear carrying a delicate bird.

Finally, they made it, choking and coughing, falling to the floor of the passageway just beyond the deluge of sand. Cazador did not follow, and it was impossible to see more than a foot into the room. Perhaps he had been buried, but Zorro doubted it.

After another minute, the sand storm thinned, then stopped entirely. Still, the haze of dust obscured the far end of the room.

Zorro stood, helped to his feet by Tanuki. As he brushed himself off, the others rose. Examining his leg, Zorros discovered that the arrowhead wound amounted to more of a bee sting than a snake bite. Still, it would be tender for a few days. Satisfied the Aztec had done no lasting damage, Zorro entered the room and looked up.

"Ingenious!" he exclaimed. The others followed his gaze. Daylight shone through the holes in the altar room's ceiling. Its rays cut bright shafts through the billowing dust. Through the holes, they could see the throne room above, which had emptied its sandy floor onto that of the room below.

Zorro limped to the back of the throne room. Cazador was nowhere to be found.

"Look at this," Zorro called, waving the others over. Yuri remained in the passage, cradling Miko in his arms while the other *ronin* entered the altar room. Ignoring a slight stinging pain, Zorro knelt before the jaguar statue on the right and grasped its feline head. "It's a lever," he told them as he pushed the statue back to its upright position. The rumbling sound repeated itself. The shafts of light from the ceiling narrowed and finally disappeared entirely.

"A pulley system, probably counterweights somewhere behind this wall, enough to slide a plate back and forth between this chamber's ceiling and the floor above." He moved the jaguar to the right once more and light returned. "Let's see what happens with this one," he said indicating the jaguar statue to the left.

Setting it upright produced a faint click, but nothing more. "Looks like this one was only meant to work once."

Washi translated Zorro's words into Japanese for Tanuki. The boy asked a question, which the older *ronin* passed on.

"What happened to the priest?"

Zorro pointed to the sand piled between the jaguar statues. The drift was considerably lower here than in the rest of the chamber. "Can you see this?" He then indicated a nearly invisible seam in the wall. Using his sword, Zorro traced the seam nearly to the ceiling, across the width between the statues and back down. "A door. Our friend Cazador is somewhere behind here. His mechanism allowed him in, but he's fixed it to keep us out."

"What is back there?" Washi asked.

Zorro stood once more. "If I remember correctly, this pyramid is built against a cliff, yes?" Washi nodded. "I would guess a warren of tunnels, chosen especially to confound pursuit." He smiled his trademark smile once more. "I'm beginning to think a cave bear is a more appropriate mascot for Cazador than his beloved jaguar."

"Shall we pursue him?" The *ronin*'s voice lacked enthusiasm.

Zorro shook his head. "No, I think it's over for

now. Cazador had been declawed, now he's defanged. You have Miko to attend to, and a comrade to bury, I believe. These are the important things, not chasing an evil priest through dark caves."

Washi became solemn, remembering Baku.

"I'm sorry about that," Zorro said with deep sincerity. "I meant to help him, but he—"

"No apology needed. He lived and died according to the code of the samurai. It is fitting." Washi would say no more.

They rejoined Yuri and Miko in the passageway. The two had been murmuring to each other in Japanese. Washi overheard a snatch of the conversation, frowned, and spoke urgently to Miko as they rose and walked up the passage. Yuri said nothing. Miko seemed to be trying to convince her leader of something. He resisted at first, then seemed to relent. The boy was following the discussion with great interest.

They were still conversing upon reaching the throne room level. Zorro looked at the great stone chair, which now sat atop a three-foot pillar. Below he could see the grate that, when closed, had held tons of sand.

Washi now spoke to Yuri, who simply nodded his head. The *ronin*'s brow wrinkled, not in displeasure, but as if entertaining a bizarre thought. He said a few words to Tanuki, who nodded eagerly.

"Tanuki and I go to bury our friend, Baku," Washi declared. "Then, we are off to explore the wide lands to the east." He gave a fatherly nod to Tanuki, who smiled broadly. Zorro found the expression a vast improvement over the murderous rage he'd seen there earlier.

"And Miko?" Zorro asked, already knowing the answer.

"She will stay with Yuri," he said with a trace of embarrassment.

At first, Zorro thought he would experience disappointment. He had found her so captivating. But he remembered the look in her eyes: fear. She too had been captivated by him, but not in a way that would have brought her contentment.

"I wish you the best," he told them sincerely. Then, with a wink, "You know where to find me should you be in need."

Yuri nodded, and smiled for only the third time since they'd met.

They made their way back to the entrance of the city and prepared to part ways. The sun, though bright, had not yet warmed the mountain air.

Yuri and Miko had agreed to return to the Cossack's cave for the time being. Washi and Tanuki had decided to retrieve Baku's body and bring it back to the hidden city for burial. The surroundings, they said, were much more in character for their friend than an anonymous grave in the wilderness. After that, they planned to be nomads.

"I return to Los Angeles, my friends." Zorro saluted them with his sword. The *ronin* bowed from astride their horses. "I bid you all a safe journey."

"You've restored our own sense of honor," Washi replied. "We will forever be in your debt, Zorro." The *ronin* leader gave a deep, respectful bow that was soon duplicated by Tanuki. After a few warm words to Miko in Japanese, the two also bowed to Yuri, then rode away to find the body of their fallen comrade. Zorro shook Yuri's hand and turned toward Miko. She was huddled in the Cossack's arms and did not look up.

"Take care of her," Zorro said.

Yuri only nodded solemnly, turned Miko's horse and the two rode away.

Zorro watched their figures recede into the distance. He then gave a last look at the hidden city and urged Tornado toward Los Angeles. The horse seemed eager to return, breaking into a gallop right away. Zorro reined him back a bit.

"There's no hurry, my friend," he told Tornado cheerfully. "Don Diego de la Vega would not be expected to rise for several hours. Let us relax and enjoy the brisk morning air." He then smiled to himself. "And take the time to think of explanations for Don Diego's rather haggard appearance and various injuries." He ticked off possibilities in his head. "A duel? No, not in Don Diego's character. Up all night studying metallurgy and struck by a shard of metal when it cooled improperly and exploded? That might have merit." Tornado trotted, oblivious to—or ignoring—his master's musings. "We'll think of something," Zorro said finally and fell silent.

He looked into the sky, delighting in the beautiful azure color streaked by wispy, white clouds. Two parallel bands of clouds appeared crossed at an angle by a third streak of white. He would swear the mark of Zorro hovered in the sky above him.

Smiling, Zorro breathed deep of the clean desert air the during the leisurely ride back to Los Angeles.